The Butterfly Key

Andrew D. Neudecker

Andrew D. Neudecker

The Butterfly Key

Copyright © 2010 by Andrew D. Neudecker

ISBN 978-0-615-37836-7

Printed in USA by Butterfly Publishing Press

Book edited by Corrine Charais

Cover design by Ted Crandall

Interior design by Andrew D. Neudecker

Author can be contacted at: thebutterflykey@yahoo.com

Dedication

For my beautiful wife

May you never have to experience the terrible tragedy of a miscarriage again, nor endure the heartbreaking loss of your faith in God a second time.

However, if by some small chance you stray off the path and find yourself lost again, simply ask me to read you this story as I did once before, and know with all of your heart and all of your soul, that as long as I am with you, you will never be alone.

This story is written for you with unconditional love. May it be your lighthouse on those dark nights, to guide you safely home to me.

Acknowledgments

To my family and friends:

There are so many people I need to thank for making this novel possible. When I said I wanted to write this story for my wife after her miscarriage, I received so much wonderful help and advice. I am indebted to all who played a part in the many aspects of this book: from the alpha and beta readers, to the people editing and giving me their feedback. There are too many names to list here, but believe me when I say I am grateful to all of you.

And to

Corrine Charais, my editor. Thank you so much for your wisdom, guidance and patience and for truly understanding the meaning behind this story. And thank you also for shaping this book into not only something beautiful, but also something extraordinary.

Also

To anyone who takes time to read this novel:

Thank you. I hope you find this a beautiful story and can appreciate the message I wanted my wife to understand: *God has a plan in all He does, even the heartrending events in life.*

Prologue

Downy snowflakes the size of cotton balls fluttered from the heavens on that unforgettable December evening. With the help of a light wind blowing in from the northwest, the snow swirled around like the soft exhale of an angel's breath, coating our entire neighborhood in a delicate, glistening fluff. My quaint house, nestled on the odd side of the street, was draped in a pristine cloak of white and puffs of smoke ascending from my chimney dissipated as they rose heavenward into the starless night.

Inside, Irving Berlin's "White Christmas" streamed from the radio, falling delightfully on my ears. I breathed in through my nose and smiled. My olfactory sense sprang to life, aroused by old familiar smells reminding me of my late grandparents' home during the holiday season. I closed my eyes and inhaled deeply, awakening long-forgotten memories of when I was a little boy. The special blends of pleasant odors filled every nook and cranny of my home. A heavy tang of pine lingered in the family room and the scent of candy cane candles filled the living room. From the kitchen, the delectable aroma of ham dinner, with just a hint of pineapple, wafted in the air. On the counter, a fresh pot of coffee was in the works. But the coffee wasn't the only thing brewing on this Christmas Eve. Tension loomed thick in the air, simmering, close to boiling over. I could sense it. I could almost taste it. Trouble was coming. This I knew.

My wife and children were on a collision course, akin to two trains hurtling toward one another, and I was stuck in the middle, tied to the tracks, so to speak. I took in a deep breath and braced myself, biding my time, awaiting their foreseeable impact. Not surprisingly, I didn't have to wait long.

My wife Nicole and I had just finished our dinner with our trio of daughters. A delightful meal it was indeed. The girls–Ashley, age fifteen; Emma, age twelve; and Chloe, a precocious age three–thought otherwise and let their mother know. By now, I was livid with my brood. They'd been testing my patience all day with their attitudes toward their mother, and this was the final straw. My wife had slaved the entire day, preparing and cooking our meal, and now she was crying, almost inconsolable. My three daughters' cutting words and their unpleasant dispositions upset me, and I banished the lot of them to their rooms while I pondered an appropriate punishment.

Normally after dinner we would all move to the family room to enjoy the roaring fire, passing out presents from underneath our beautiful Christmas tree. But this Christmas I found my wife sitting on the couch next to the fireplace, sobbing. She was petting her always-faithful cat, who was sitting on her lap purring with loud contentment. This large orange cat was more like a gentle lion. His paws were huge, his whiskers long, and his fur trimmed with a lion's cut. He was the one true friend my wife could always depend upon to listen when I couldn't be around.

Christmas Eve in my household is a day of relaxation and giving. My three daughters, on the other hand, had made it anything but. Taking a deep breath, I walked over behind my wife. I said nothing as I massaged her neck, working to help ease and unwind her frayed nerves. My wife was still distraught over the miscarriage of our baby almost a year earlier. On top of that, I knew her faith in God had been faltering day after day. It didn't take much effort on our children's part to put my wife into a state of sorrowful distress. However, between the cat and I, we were able to soothe her soul with our infinite love. As I walked around the couch and sat down, I looked to my wife and smiled. We sat in silence for a few minutes, gazing upon the soft glow of the fireplace. Even though we were both quiet, my mind labored, diligent in trying to think of a suitable punishment for my daughters that would resonate toughness, love, and the giving spirit of Christmas. I also was searching for a way to help my wife establish her faith in God once again.

While pondering, I looked over to all the wrapped gifts underneath our tree and an idea dawned on me, as if someone just turned on a light. Right there in my own living room, I had an epiphany!

With a loud thunder in my voice, I called out my three ill-behaved daughters' names. "Ashley, Emma, Chloe, get your butts in the living room now!" My voice rumbled like a freight train throughout the house, and to this day, my daughters swear the walls of the house shook when I bellowed out their names. When the trio arrived in the living room, I told them to take a seat on the couch with their mother. They knew it was time to face my ire.

The three of them sat in silence beside their mother, cowering in fear. I focused my dark, penetrating eyes on each one of them in turn. The last thing they should've done was make their mother upset, and they knew it. My glare was more than enough, because I didn't have to castigate them with the harsh words dancing on the tip of my tongue. Their apologies were prompt and simultaneous, and they hugged their mother with a remorseful fervor. When they finished seeking her forgiveness, I demanded their complete and utmost attention.

I pointed to the mountain of presents piled all around our Christmas tree and, tersely, I gave them my ultimatum. Grounding them for a week along with having all their gifts donated to charity was my punishment of choice. They bemoaned this option as soon as I uttered the words. Therefore, I offered them an alternative punishment: to listen to me with all their hearts as I would tell them a story over the next few hours. This, however, I told them, was no ordinary story, and if they failed to listen, I would levy my first punishment without compunction. They sat in silence as I continued to tell them this would be a story of love, loss, faith, determination, sacrifice, and purpose. A story of two families forever intertwined by fate: Christian, Elizabeth and Noah Bryson, and Abigail, Alexander, Ian, and Isabelle Havily.

My daughters were wise and elected option two. My wife smiled, delighted with their choice, while the cat purred, content that my wife was stroking the orange fur right between his ears.

"So be it then," I said. I sat down in my comfortable, brown, oversized chair. My eyes rested on my now-attentive progeny and wife. Then, guided by something I can only consider extraordinary, I began to narrate the tragic but miraculous yarn of the Bryson and Havily families, which in hindsight changed everything for my wife, for my children, and for me.

Chapter 1

FLASHBACK: INDEPENDENCE DAY — SOME TWENTY YEARS EARLIER

"Noah, I love you always, my husband," Elizabeth said, her faint voice barely even a whisper.

"And I love you, too. Take it easy, my love, and try not to overdo it. You need to get some rest now. You've had a very difficult delivery," Noah replied, his tender voice nothing more than a hushed murmur. Trying to put on a brave face, he sat down in a chair beside Elizabeth's hospital bed. He took her hands into his own and caressed them, rubbing soft circles with his thumbs.

Noah remained shaken, fraught with worry over his wife's traumatic ordeal and her now-fragile appearance. The birth of their child, a son, was anything but a normal delivery. It started with sixteen hours of intense hard labor and ended with an emergency c-section with a major loss of blood.

Elizabeth's face had grown pale and looked exhausted, as if she'd weathered the storm of a hundred lifetimes. Her glassy-green eyes were vibrant as emeralds, and yet they somehow seemed stained by a dark, indelible ink. She struggled to focus on Noah's eyes in the room's unpleasant light.

Noah continued to caress Elizabeth's soft hands, and though doing this eased her some, it did nothing to quell the feeling of hopelessness deep inside his heart. Noah struggled to watch his beautiful wife be in so much pain, and he felt powerless to help her.

"Please call Ian and Isabelle for me," Elizabeth whispered. This time her weak voice was much stronger than before. "I need to see them tonight."

Noah brushed her soft brown hair away from her eyes with a gentle touch. "They're already on their way, my love. I called them while you were being moved from surgery to your room. They should be here soon."

"Thank you."

"You're welcome, my love."

Elizabeth and Isabelle had been best friends since they were kids. Elizabeth served as Isabelle's maid of honor when she married Ian; Isabelle returned the favor, serving as the matron of honor when Elizabeth married Noah a few years later.

Noah and Elizabeth didn't have to wait long before Ian and Isabelle arrived. Isabelle waddled in first, six months pregnant, carrying twins. Ian followed on her heels, making quacking sounds to accent the fact that his wife walked like a duck.

"Knock that off!" Isabelle said, giving Ian a punch on his arm.

Noah chuckled to himself. He couldn't help but think how Isabelle and Elizabeth were alike in so many ways.

"I'm sorry we're late, Elizabeth. Ian was working on his sermon for next Sunday's service and I had to swing by the church to pick him up," Isabelle explained.

Ian, the priest of a local Anglican church in town, had presided over the marriage between Noah and Elizabeth just a few years before.

Both Isabelle and Ian gave Elizabeth a giant hug, and then one to Noah.

"We're so happy for you both," Ian said.

"Thank you," Noah replied, smiling.

"Have you decided on a name?" Isabelle asked.

"Christian," Elizabeth replied softly.

Isabelle's eyes twinkled. "Oh, that's beautiful! When can I see him?"

"Noah," Elizabeth asked her husband, "would you please take Isabelle to see our son?"

"Yes, my love."

Elizabeth turned her attention to Ian. "Please sit with me. I am in need of your spiritual guidance."

Ian smiled at Elizabeth and sat down on the edge of her hospital bed. "I'm here for you, my dear," he said, taking her hand.

"We'll be back in a little while, you two," Noah said, excitement radiating from his face. He put his arm around Isabelle and said, "Let's go see my son."

* * *

"Now then, what's on your mind?" Ian asked Elizabeth.

"I need you to do three things for me." Elizabeth struggled to sit up as she spoke, a hint of desperation clung to her words. "You must promise to do them. You must!"

"I promise," Ian said, surprised at the urgent tone in her voice. "What is it you need?"

Elizabeth stared deep into Ian's eyes, and he knew she was serious: dead serious, to be exact. Taking a deep breath and giving his hand a firm squeeze, Elizabeth began.

"First, there's a gift in my suitcase. It's for my son, and I want you to give it to him when the time comes. Ian reached down and retrieved the box, wrapped with red paper and a gold bow.

"When am I supposed to give it to him?"

"When he has children of his own," she answered.

A look of confusion came over Ian's face. He didn't understand why she was asking him to do this.

"This is your son. You can give this to him yourself."

Elizabeth sighed, and then whispered, "Oh Ian, you'll understand soon enough." Gathering her strength, she continued, "The second thing I need you to do is help Noah raise Christian. He'll need your guidance."

A wave of sadness engulfed Ian, penetrating and darkening his soul like an eclipse. The realization of what Elizabeth was asking started to dawn on him. Ian fought to steady himself. He tightened his lips and nodded, not trusting himself to speak. He had to compose himself; she needed him to be strong now.

"Please don't be afraid for me, Ian, for I am not." A peaceful undertone echoed in her faint voice. "I'm going to serve, for a greater good, a higher purpose. You'll understand in time. And I promise you this; we'll see each other again someday. You can count on it."

Ian released Elizabeth's hand and stood up. He glanced over to the bedside table and stared at the bible sitting atop it. He recognized it immediately. He and Isabelle had given it to Elizabeth and Noah for a wedding gift. Ian looked back and smiled at Elizabeth.

"You don't need to ask me the third question. I already know what you need of me."

Elizabeth looked over at the bible, then back at Ian, and nodded, as if she were telling him to proceed.

Ian picked up the bible and held it in his hands for a moment. His breath was deep and deliberate as he worked to compose himself. He opened the bible and thumbed through the pages, locating the page he didn't want to find. He paused a second, then began to administer last rights to Elizabeth.

* * *

Noah and Isabelle stared into the nursery through the protective glass.

"Is that him, Noah?"

"Yes!" he replied, unable to contain his excitement. "That's my son."

"Christian is so beautiful. I'm so happy for both of you." Isabelle rubbed her own tummy, and contentment washed across her face as she envisioned her own children's impending birth. "A few more short months and I will be a mom, too," she thought to herself.

"Thank you. Would you like to hold him?"

"Would I ever!" she said, clapping her hands together.

"Okay then, let's do it."

Noah knocked on the secured nursery door, and the head nurse let them in. He motioned for Isabelle to sit down in the rocking chair in the corner. The nurse swaddled Christian in a receiving blanket and handed him to Isabelle.

Isabelle's eyes widened, filled with amazement as she cradled Christian in her arms. She rocked him, slow and steady, whispering to him with her soft voice.

"He's so perfect in every way," she said, her eyes admiring God's precious gift.

"I'm glad you think so. You're going to make an excellent godmother."

"Really? Oh my gosh, thank you. I feel honored."

As Isabelle rocked Christian, she thought about how she would soon need both arms to hold her twins.

Before long Noah looked at his wristwatch and said, "I think we should be getting back now. I'm concerned about Elizabeth."

Isabelle motioned for the nurse to take Christian from her. Once the nurse had the baby in her arms, Noah helped Isabelle up from the rocking chair and escorted her out of the nursery.

When Noah and Isabelle arrived back at Elizabeth's room, they found Ian standing in the doorway, his head hanging low. He clung onto the gift Elizabeth had given him to one day bestow upon Christian. An unmistakable, deep, depressed look enveloped his face, as if someone had just sapped all the life from his soul.

"What in the heavens is wrong, Ian?" asked Isabelle, her voice filled with concern.

Ian didn't respond at first, trying to muster the strength to answer. After a moment, he looked at his wife with tears in his eyes, and then to Noah and said, "Go be with your wife. There's not much time left." The sorrow exuding from deep within Ian's red-rimmed, puffy eyes darkened Noah and Isabelle's cheerfulness like a moonless night.

Noah's face shifted from happiness to horror in a heartbeat. Total disbelief overwhelmed him as he rushed into his wife's room and held her, hoping this was nothing more than a terrible nightmare.

Isabelle tried to follow but Ian grabbed her by the arm. "Let them be alone," he said, his voice echoing the sorrow his eyes had already delivered. Ian put his arms around his pregnant wife and whispered into her ear, "They need whatever short time is left to be together, alone."

Isabelle closed her eyes and began to shake, sobbing hard in her husband's arms. Ian held her tight and said nothing else. He just held onto his wife in the long hospital hallway as they waited for the inevitable.

Elizabeth's face had turned sallow, and her weary eyes had grown darker. It would not be long until her fast-fading spirit would float away, much like the snowy white parachutes of once-yellow dandelions, taking their final dances in the delicate kisses of the summer winds.

Noah did not fight his emotions. He sobbed as he held Elizabeth in his trembling arms. She put her hand on the back of his neck, caressing it with slow, deliberate strokes.

"You're a wonderful husband and you'll make a wonderful father to our son," she said. A passionate determination graced her face.

"I don't want to do it without you!" Noah's voice cracked under the tremendous weight of heartache. "I don't have the strength or will."

"You're so much stronger than you think you are, my love. Know this with all your heart. You will never be alone." Her voice was fading, growing fainter with each shallow breath she took. "I love you always and forever," Elizabeth murmured. She squeezed the back of her devoted husband's neck with the last ounce of her strength.

Elizabeth's limp hand slipped away from Noah's head and fell to her side, her determination vanishing with her strength. She didn't have the willpower to fight anymore. She took one last breath and smiled at her husband with adoring eyes. Then, she closed her eyes and passed away, embarking on what would be her remarkable journey to her greater purpose.

Noah touched his wife's still-warm cheeks, cupping them in his hands. He leaned over and kissed her one last time. "I love you always, Elizabeth, always," he said. Then, Noah put his head down onto her lifeless body and cried, while his trembling hands stroked her long, soft, brown hair.

Chapter 2

HOMECOMING:
LATE JUNE - SOME TWENTY YEARS LATER

Columbus Township, Minnesota. The small, tight-knit community situated just a few miles west of Forest Lake, a quick thirty-five minute drive north of the Twin Cities, was the only place Christian Bryson and Alexander Havily, best friends for their whole lives, had ever called home.

Both young men were twenty years old. Christian stood about five feet eleven inches tall, with short black hair and hazel eyes. His skin's tone was a fair milky-white. Alexander was much tanner than Christian, but an inch or so shorter. His eyes and hair were shaded a soft brown. Both young men possessed lean and muscular body frames, as they each had played both football and baseball when they were in high school.

Christian lived with his father, Noah, just down the road from Alexander's home. Alexander lived with his parents, Ian and Isabelle, and his twin sister Abigail.

Christian and Abigail's love was deep and passionate. They had been an item for the past seven years, but their affinity for one another started blossoming when they were still in diapers. Neither one had ever dated anyone else, nor had they ever had the desire to. Soon the sweet sound of wedding bells would toll for them both; it was only a matter of time.

Christian and Alexander felt both tired and excited. They were heading home after two exhaustive weeks of Minnesota Army National Guard training. Based out of Stillwater, they belonged to the 34th "Red Bull" infantry division, attached to the 34th military police company.

"Christian, you're pretty quiet today. Is everything okay?" Alexander asked as he turned down the car radio.

"I just have a lot on my mind and I'm tired," Christian replied. The somber tone in his voice did nothing to hide the fact that his mind was somewhere else, a place overflowing with concern.

"I can offer a penny for your thoughts," Alexander said. "We have about twenty minutes before we get home."

"I'm just worried about my dad. He wasn't looking too good before we left for our training."

Noah's cancer had remained in remission for just over a year now, but the once-strong man was now ever-so-frail as he battled his arch enemy, cancer.

"I wish I could do more for him. My dad doesn't talk about his cancer with me at all, so the not-knowing part is very hard on me."

Alexander nodded to Christian to let him know he understood. He wanted to help his friend but he knew deep down that listening was the only thing he could do.

Alexander changed the subject to something that would make Christian much happier. "So, what's up with you and Abigail?" The tone in Alexander's voice made it sound as if he were grilling Christian.

"What do you mean?" Christian replied. He squirmed in his driver's seat like a worm on a fishhook.

"You know exactly what I mean!" Alexander prodded. "When are you going to propose to my sister? You know she is dying to spend the rest of her life with you!"

"I know, Alexander, I know. And honestly, between you and me, I'm going to talk to my dad about it later today when we get home."

"That's awesome! I believe you two will be happy together."

"Thank you, Alexander. You're a very good friend."

The rest of the drive home was rather uneventful. Alexander turned the radio back to the country station and both young men lost themselves in their thoughts.

* * *

Christian turned into the driveway of Alexander and Abigail's home. The setting was magnificent. On each side, a towering weeping willow tree stood at attention, as if standing guard, keeping a watchful eye on all who came and went. Both young men marveled at the beauty of the property as they approached the house. Tall, majestic old oak trees lined each side of the long driveway.

Christian parked the truck and both young men stepped out onto the gravel driveway. A sweet fragrance hung in the air.

"Alexander, it looks like your mom and Abigail have been busy tending to the flower garden." Christian's eyes surveyed the landscape, impressed by the picture-perfect beauty laid out before him.

"Yeah, I know. All these flowers look and smell amazing."

The house was an old two-and-a-half-story Queen Anne, which Alexander's parents had recently refurbished with new olive green siding and dark shingles. All the windows were new, accented with dark green trim, and the woodwork on the doorway around the three-quarter stained glass front door was painted to match the window trim. A tower on the left side of the house stretched high into the sky. A white porch wrapped around both sides of the home, and a reddish cobblestone sidewalk stretched from the gravel driveway all the way up to the front porch steps. A colorful assortment of shrubbery and flowers planted in front of the home made it even more inviting.

The front door swung open and Abigail stepped out onto the porch. She was petite, barely five feet tall, and couldn't weigh more than a hundred pounds. Abigail's hair was shoulder length, light brown, and very curly. She wore a pair of blue Levi's jean shorts and a pink tank top.

Christian caught sight of her as she came down the porch steps. As she stepped into the sunlight, her light blue eyes sparkled, and he could see the excitement in them. Two weeks away from him was much more than she ever wanted to bear.

Abigail raced to him and jumped into his arms with reckless abandon, then squeezed him tight, as if to let him know he must never leave her again.

"I missed you so much!" Abigail cooed, planting a tender kiss on his soft lips.

"I missed you, too," Christian replied.

"God, I love you," Abigail said, kissing his lips again.

Christian tried in vain to say "I love you" back, but Abigail's soft lips pressed hard into his, making it almost impossible to breathe, let alone speak.

"Hey, get a room, for crying out loud!" Alexander shouted, his booming voice interrupting their reunion.

"Shut up, you goon!" Abigail bellowed. She gave her twin brother a wicked slug in the arm, then hugged him. "I'm glad you're home, too."

"It's good to see you, too, Sissy," he said in a teasing tone.

Alexander walked to the back of Christian's truck and retrieved his army duffle bag, allowing Abigail to return her attention to Christian. She walked over, embraced him again, and purred into his ear, "God, I love a man in uniform."

"It's good to see you boys made it back home," an old familiar voice rang out from the porch steps.

An elegant and beautiful woman walked gracefully down the cobblestone path to greet them. She was taller than Abigail, but not by much, and if you didn't know any better you could easily mistake them for sisters.

"Hello Mom!" Alexander said, giving her a hug. "It's good to see you. Any chance you're cooking us dinner tonight?"

"Does the army not feed you at all?" Isabelle quipped, laughing at her son.

"Nowhere near as good as you do, Mom."

Isabelle just smiled and then looked over to Christian. "Can I tear you away from my daughter long enough so I can get a hug from you, too?"

"Sure thing, Mom." Christian gave Isabelle a long, affectionate hug. He had called her "Mom" for as long as he could remember. She and Ian had helped Noah raise him after his mom died, and Christian was fond of his surrogate parents and happy they were in his life.

"So, are you just as hungry as the human garbage disposal I have for a son?"

"Yes, ma'am. I am," Christian replied.

"Good," Isabelle said. "Dinner will be served at six sharp. Let your dad know I'm cooking one of his favorite meals: my famous tacos. Whatever you do, don't be late."

Christian nodded that he understood. "We won't be. My dad can't resist your cooking, and neither can I."

"Well then, I'd better get started straight away." Isabelle turned and went back to the house, shouting as she went through the door. "Six sharp!"

Christian watched Isabelle go into the house and shut the door. Refocusing his attention back on Abigail, he looked long and deep into her light blue eyes. "There's something I'm thinking about asking you later tonight," he said, holding Abigail's hands. "But I need to run home first and clean up and check on my dad."

"Don't you want to ask me now, my love?" Abigail bit her lower lip and batted her long eyelashes.

"Not a chance! You're just going to have to wait."

"Oh, all right," Abigail pouted. She wanted to know what he had to say, but he wouldn't budge.

Christian gave Abigail a kiss, winked at her, and slid into his truck. He rolled down the window and smiled. "I love you. I'll see you later this evening." Then to Alexander, "You too."

Alexander nodded to his friend, and Abigail mouthed the words "I love you" as Christian put his truck into gear and drove down the driveway. Abigail waved to Christian until she could no longer hear the gravel crunching underneath his truck tires.

When Christian disappeared from sight, Alexander slung his duffle bag over his left shoulder and put his right arm around his sister, escorting her up the cobblestone sidewalk and porch steps to their house.

Alexander laughed, his smile beaming from ear to ear. "Tonight will be an interesting dinner engagement."

"You think so?" Abigail asked, with hesitance.

"No, I know. I just know."

Alexander then opened up the stained glass front door for his sister. "Ladies first," he said, tipping his military cap to her.

"You're so thoughtful." Abigail walked inside the house, her stride graceful, and Alexander followed her in, shutting the door behind him.

Chapter 3

FATHER AND SON

The drive to his home from Abigail's took less than sixty seconds. The distance was a little over half a mile. Christian parked his truck in the driveway, then stepped out and walked to the rear of the vehicle to retrieve his army green duffle bag. As he glanced back at the road, he lost himself in thought.

For years, that road was a path to Abigail, the first, only, and quite definitely the last girl he would ever kiss. Christian reminisced about how his love for her had grown throughout the years, as if he planted an acorn into the fertile ground and watched it develop into a strong, beautiful oak tree. Their love, too, was rooted deep and branching out to the furthest reaches of the sky, still growing bit by bit with each passing day.

When Christian was younger, he would walk to her house in the wintertime. To him, it seemed like it took an eternity to get to her. For this reason, Christian didn't care for winter. The other three seasons Christian could ride his bicycle, but even then, it still seemed like it took forever to reach her, no matter how hard he peddled. Now, even with his truck, his short journey to her still seemed like it lasted a lifetime.

"Man, I have it bad," he muttered under his breath, shaking his head in wonderment as he grabbed his duffle bag and headed to the front door of his dad's house. The home was nothing spectacular, just a modest three-bedroom rambler, painted white, situated on one acre of land, with apple trees surrounding it and a white picket fence encompassing them both. Simple, yet practical, as it provided Christian and his dad with everything they needed.

They moved in when Christian was three years old. Their previous home near the Carlos Avery game farm had burned to the ground in a wildfire. Christian and his father had lost everything in fire: clothes, furniture, photographs, and most other personal belongings. When they moved here, they had nothing except each other, and for Christian, this was enough.

Christian's dad had raised him with love and never-ending patience and had taught him discipline and grace. If you were to peel away all the layers, all the trials and tribulations, and all the tragedies in his life, Noah was a good dad, trying his best to play the hand life had dealt him.

"Dad, I'm home!" Christian shouted as he walked through the front door.

"I'm in the kitchen!" Noah yelled back.

Christian set his duffle bag down in the entryway and proceeded to the kitchen. His dad sat at the table, reading the local newspaper. Christian paused, then breathed in something wonderful, a familiar, delicate aroma that made his mouth water. Christian knew what his father was baking. The aroma had been etched into his mind since he was a child.

"Homemade apple pie," he sighed as he exhaled.

"Is there any other kind?" Noah rhetorically questioned. "I picked apples off the trees in the backyard earlier today."

"I see retirement is treating you very well, old man. You're a regular old Betty Crocker now."

Noah chuckled. "Yeah, I guess I am."

Christian's dad had turned fifty a few months earlier, but he looked much older than his years. Noah's hair, what little he still possessed, was white. His body was now fragile, and his constitution delicate. Bone cancer had devastated this once-strong man, reducing him to a mere shadow of his former self. Noah had become dependant on a walking cane, which he hated with a passion. He needed to have it or he wouldn't be able to walk, but the cane was an albatross that weighed on his resolve relentlessly, day after grueling day.

Noah thought himself a helpless cripple, but he was far from that. He had a sharp mind, an outstanding memory, and a quick wit. The one thing this ravenous cancer could never do was devastate his large, passionate heart. He was far too strong for that. Noah was the ultimate die-hard: never wavering, hopelessly romantic, and passionate about life and love. A fighter he always would be until the bitter end. However, Noah was deadlocked in a pernicious game of chess with the cancer, and for the time being, both masters would have to settle for a stalemate in their battle between life and death.

Christian looked over to the clock on the wall. The time: a quarter to five. He walked over to the kitchen table, pulled out a chair, and sat down.

"Dad, are you busy?"

"Not at all," he replied, closing his newspaper.

"Do you have a minute or two to talk?"

"Sure, son, I have a little time. Tell me what's on your mind, but make it quick. As you can see, I have apple pies baking in the oven that I don't want to burn."

Christian started to speak. "I …" he paused for a long moment, thinking of the right words to say to his dad.

"Spit it out, son!" Noah playfully shouted.

"I want to get married!"

Noah raised his eyebrows and stared at his son for a good ten seconds before responding. "Son, I love you, but I believe what you're asking is not even legal in this state. Besides, I don't think I'm your type."

Christian fell silent, speechless at his dad's response. Then it dawned on him, his words hadn't come out right. "I want to get married to Abigail, you moron!"

Noah laughed, hearty and deep. "Yeah, I know. You just looked so tense so I figured I would lighten the mood. Well, I must say, it's about damn time. When are you going to ask her?"

"I think I want to do it this evening, but maybe tomorrow would be better."

"There's an old adage I live by when I hear people tell me they're going to do things tomorrow."

"Which is what, Dad?"

"Too many tomorrows add up to a lot of empty yesterdays."

Christian pondered his father's advice for a moment, then decided his father was right and he shouldn't put off any longer what his heart had yearned for all these years.

Christian, his eyes dancing, looked at his father. "Okay then. How about I do it tonight? Isabelle has invited us over for dinner at six, and she said I must bring you."

Noah looked long and hard at Christian before responding. "Well then, let me give you some advice about Abigail's parents before we head over there. First, they're somewhat old fashioned, so I suggest you ask permission to marry their only daughter. Second, you might want to get upstairs and shower. You stink. Also, put on a shirt and tie."

Noah's third piece of advice involved Abigail. "Always tell Abigail you love her no matter what and cherish every moment you two have together. Son, you just never know what will happen, because sometimes life can be cold and cruel. Death can steal love away from you in a mere heartbeat without any cause or warning. It could happen today, it could happen tomorrow, it could never happen at all. But if it does, you'll carry no regrets, just happy memories of the never-ending love you have for one another."

Christian knew his dad was talking about his mother, a subject quickly changed when he asked his dad about her. Noah was a very private man, and his memories were just that, his own. He never remarried, never even went out on a date again after Elizabeth died. Christian's birthdays were bittersweet for Noah: A day of celebrating another year of his son's life, but also a day that served as a cruel reminder of his wife's death. Every year Noah would light another candle on his son's birthday cake, and every year after Christian went to bed, Noah would faithfully light a candle in Elizabeth's memory, then lose himself to the darkness of the night.

Christian shook his father's arm, rousting him from his memories of long ago. "Dad, you were lost in thought. Are you all right?" he asked with caution, not knowing what to expect next.

"I'm fine, son. Sorry about that. I was just thinking about how beautiful your mother was."

"I wish I carried those memories of Mom, too, Dad. I'm sorry you lost everything of hers when the house burned down."

Christian had never seen the scores of pictures his father had possessed of his mother before the wildfire took them. The only pictures of his mother he could remember seeing were photographs taken of her as a child and teenager, which adorned the walls of his grandparents' house. He'd never seen a photograph of his mother as an adult. She died at the young age of twenty-seven.

"I didn't lose everything, Christian. I still have our…" he paused, looked at his son and quickly changed the subject.

Christian wanted to know what his dad meant, but he knew his father all too well. Any attempt to find out any information at all would be futile.

Noah refocused his attention on his son. "When do you have to go over there for dinner?"

"*We,*" Christian said, scolding his dad. "We have to go over there at six or Isabelle will have my butt. So if I have to pick you up and carry you there, I will. Besides, it would be nice to have you there when I make a complete fool out of myself."

"Well, I wouldn't want you to get into trouble with Isabelle. I know how feisty that woman can be. Ian has his hands full with her. Moreover, it might be fun and entertaining to watch you squirm just a little bit."

"I do appreciate your desire to watch me suffer."

"Don't mention it," Noah said, teasing his son. "You'll do just fine. Trust me. Everything will work out just fine. It always does."

Noah leaned over, put his hand on Christian's shoulder, and shook it. A look of utmost pride filled Noah's eyes, knowing he had raised a fine young man.

"So, son, let me see it."

"See what?"

"The engagement ring… you know… the thing you're going to put on Abigail's finger when you get down on your knee and propose to her."

A long and awkward silence hung in the air. Noah burst out in laughter. He knew his son hadn't purchased an engagement ring.

"Oh damn!" Christian said, smacking his forehead in disbelief.

"Relax, son, and listen to me. We need to work fast," Noah said, looking at the clock on the kitchen wall. "One hour until show time. I want you to go upstairs and get yourself cleaned up. Meet me over at Abigail's place at six and be ready to rock and roll."

"But, Dad, what about the engagement ring?" A hint of desperation resonated in Christian's voice.

"I'll take care of that. You're lucky Bear and I are friends."

"Who the hell is Bear?" Christian asked, not sure if he wanted to know.

"Bear is the owner of the jewelry store in town. He owes me a few favors from over the years, and it's time I cashed them in. I'll get you what they call a loner ring. It's just a simple diamond engagement ring you can use to propose to Abigail. Then tomorrow you can go back to the jewelry store with Abigail and let her pick out her dream ring."

"Wow! Thanks, Dad."

Noah nodded and smiled. "Now get moving. No time to spare."

Christian ran out of the kitchen to get himself ready for his future. Noah watched him leave the room and laughed to himself. Then he stood up, using the cane he loathed so much.

His bones ached as he ambled over to the stove and put on an oven mitt. He opened the oven door, steam spewing out as he did so, and removed two homemade apple pies. He put them on the counter to cool, turned off the oven, and tossed the oven mitt on the counter. Then Noah picked up his car keys and walked gingerly out the door.

Chapter 4

THE DINNER ENGAGEMENT

"Isabelle, I'm home!" Ian called out, closing the stained glass door behind him.

"We're all in the kitchen!" she called back.

Ian set down his briefcase, removed his dress shoes, and put on his slippers. It had been a long day at the church, and he had looked forward to coming home to spend time with his family.

Ian was in his fifties, but didn't look a day over forty. His frame was lean and slender. He kept himself in good shape with a balanced work-out regimen, running three to five miles every day. His once jet-black hair had long since turned silver, and his eyes were a deep blue, like lapis lazuli.

Ian walked through the house to the kitchen. It appeared his family was busy preparing dinner. He spotted Abigail and Isabelle cutting tomatoes on the cutting board. Alexander was frying up some hamburger meat on the stovetop.

"Hello, son," Ian said, delighted to see Alexander home from reserve training.

"Hey, Dad," Alexander replied, waving his spatula.

"Tacos!" Ian said. "This could mean only one thing. I guess we're having Noah and Christian over for dinner tonight."

"We can't get anything by you, can we, Dad?" Abigail teased.

Ian rubbed his hands together. "Well then, what can I do to help?"

"Would you be a darling and set the dinner table?" Isabelle asked.

"I'm on it, my dear."

The doorbell chimed a sweet melodious tone that reverberated throughout the house.

"I'll get it," Isabelle said, setting down her knife. As she walked to the front door, she glanced at the antique clock hanging by the entryway. Almost six o'clock now. Isabelle opened up the door to see Christian standing on the porch, wearing black dress pants, a white dress shirt, and a black tie. His hair was combed and his face clean shaven. A sweet fragrance floated around Christian: Polo cologne, his weapon of choice.

"Well, don't you look debonair this evening, Christian," Isabelle said, blocking the doorway.

"Thank you. May I please come in?"

Isabelle stood steadfast in the door's opening, preventing Christian from entering. She glared at him, a look Christian knew all too well. This was her ominous warning he had done something terribly wrong.

"Where's your dad?" she questioned in a voice that breathed a hint of indignation. "Did you forget to bring him?"

"Umm, no," he replied uneasily. Christian fought to stand his ground under her gaze. "Dad had to run a few errands in town first. He said he'd be here for dinner."

Just then, right as Christian thought he would buckle under Isabelle's intense gaze, his father's car came into view as it rolled down the driveway.

"I guess this is your lucky day." She stepped aside to let him into the house.

"Do you mean to tell me you weren't going to let me in without my dad?"

"I guess we'll find out next time, won't we?" she replied, a devilish look dancing on her face.

Christian entered the house, sidestepping Isabelle. He thought to himself she was one woman he would never want to upset. He couldn't tell if she was serious. Being a lawyer for many years had perfected her poker face. Christian knew he could never bluff her. He didn't even want to try.

Isabelle stepped onto the porch, and waited for Noah to come up the steps. He limped at a slow, painful pace, the hated cane in his right hand, tapping on the cobblestone sidewalk as he approached.

"You're late!" she confronted him, her hands on her hips.

Noah looked at his watch. One minute after six. He knew there'd be hell to pay. "Aw come on!" Noah pleaded his case. "I'm only a minute late!"

"That still means you're late. It also means if you want to eat my delicious cooking, you'll have to wash dishes with my husband after dinner."

"What's for dinner?"

"We're having tacos," she replied. Isabelle knew all too well she had Noah wrapped around her little finger by making his favorite meal.

"Mmm, okay. You've got a deal," he said, extending his hand to Isabelle. She extended hers back and they shook on it. "You drive a hard bargain. You're lucky I love your amazing cooking, also the pleasant company of the rest of your family."

Isabelle busted out with laughter, and so did Noah. The dear old friends hugged each other and laughed until tears rolled down their cheeks.

The two families sat down to enjoy dinner and conversation at the elegant, beautiful antique oak dining room table, a staple in the family for many years and the centerpiece of the room. Stained a rich, dark, walnut color, the table had been hand carved by a master artisan. It had been a family heirloom for years now, given to Isabelle and Ian as a wedding gift from Ian's grandparents. Ian, Isabelle, Alexander, and Abigail had gravitated to the antique table for important family discussions and decisions many times over the years, and Noah and Christian, considered family, were often included. The two families shared many fond memories together at this table, and everyone expected many more memories to come.

Ian stood and led the two families in saying grace before dinner, an hour-long light-hearted affair filled with many funny stories and memories of Christian, Alexander, and Abigail growing up. Like the many evenings before, a lot of laughs and smiles were shared this night.

When dinner was finished, Abigail, Christian, and Alexander helped Isabelle clear the table so Noah and Ian could proceed with dishwashing duty. Soon after seven, cleanup had been finished and everyone moved into the large living room.

The living room's ambience delivered a unique northern flavor. A quaint stone hearth fireplace was nestled into the corner of the room. Two large oversized chairs, a couch, and a loveseat were arranged in front of the fireplace. The walls were painted a warm light beige with an eggshell finish, and three Terry Redlin paintings, one directly over the mantel of the now-dormant fireplace, gave the room an inviting atmosphere.

Isabelle went into the kitchen to retrieve six wine glasses, while Ian went to the cellar to fetch a couple large bottles of Barefoot Mascotti. Noah and Alexander each took a seat in the comfortable, oversized chairs. Christian and Abigail positioned themselves close together on the loveseat. When

Ian and Isabelle returned, they sat down on the couch and proceeded to uncork one of the bottles of wine.

"Why don't you play us something nice, Abigail?" Ian asked his daughter while filling glasses of wine.

"Okay, Dad."

"I'll get your guitar," Alexander said. He jumped out of his chair and ran upstairs to her room.

When it came to music, Abigail possessed a remarkable gift. She'd started learning how to play the guitar at the age of five. Her singing was amazing: not by what she sang but how she sang it. If Abigail didn't believe in the words of a song with passion, she wouldn't play or sing it. Her ability to move people in inspirational and divine ways with her singing was exceptional. Every other Sunday, Abigail volunteered to sing to the residents at the nursing home in town, and when she finished, the elderly men and woman would be either smiling from ear to ear or moved to tears. For Abigail, knowing she made just one person's day more meaningful with her music filled her heart and soul with joy.

"Here you go, Sissy," Alexander said as he returned with her guitar. She thanked him, and he sat back down.

"What are you going to play?" Christian asked.

Abigail didn't say a word. She just looked at Christian, gave him a tender smile, and winked. She cradled her guitar and began to play, her fingers working effortlessly to fill the room with the tune's melody. Then she started to sing. The words rolled off her tongue with immense passion. Clearly, she had not chosen a song to entertain the group. She had picked a breathtaking, beautiful song, "A Moment Like This," to deliver a strong message to the one she loved.

Her message was very clear. Abigail was professing to Christian the profound love she had nurtured deep within and had experienced for most of her life. Everyone in the room understood from each sweet, passionate word just what she wanted: Christian. And in that fleeting moment of time, Christian, too, knew what he wanted most: Abigail. He had already grown up with her. Now he wanted to grow old with her, to experience and share everything with her for the rest of their lives together.

As she finished the song, total silence fell over the room like a curtain. Everyone was trying to take in the beautiful moment they had just experienced.

"A toast," Noah said. His deep, loud voice joyously broke the silence of the room. He raised his wine glass high. "To a moment like this. May there be many more of them to come."

"Hear, hear," they all replied, clinking their glasses and then drinking their wine.

Christian stood up and turned to Ian and Isabelle. He took a deep breath, trying to quiet his nerves, then stated in a firm voice, "Mr. and Mrs. Havily, I would like permission to marry your daughter."

Ian and Isabelle didn't have a chance to answer before Abigail jumped up in excitement and tackled Christian to the ground. She was on top of him, kissing his face all over.

"I surrender, I surrender!" he mumbled through the kisses.

Ian and Isabelle had known this day would come. They looked at each other with knowing smiles. Then Ian spoke for both of them, saying, "You have our blessing."

Abigail stood up, grabbed Christian's hands, and pulled him to his feet. Ian and Isabelle hugged them both and congratulated them on their engagement. But Alexander played the devil's advocate. "Why are you congratulating them when he hasn't put a ring on her finger?"

"That's where I come in," Noah said. He stood, with the help of his cane, and reached into his pants pocket. He pulled out a small, red jewelry box. Every eye in the room was transfixed on Noah as he limped over to Abigail and Christian. "The reason I was a little late for dinner tonight is because Christian asked me to go to the jewelry store to pick up a ring for Abigail."

"You picked out my ring?" Abigail asked.

"Heavens no," replied Noah.

"He went for me to pick up a loner engagement ring," Christian stated.

Noah shrugged his shoulders. "Um... well, not exactly."

"What?" Christian exclaimed. A look of alarm washed over his face.

"First," Noah explained, "I went to the bank and withdrew five thousand dollars. Then I drove to the jewelry store to see my friend Bear. Tomorrow morning at ten, you two kids have an appointment with Bear to pick out your wedding rings. This is my wedding gift to you."

"I don't know what to say," Abigail said in disbelief.

"A thank you would do very nicely," Noah replied.

Abigail hugged her soon-to-be father-in-law, then kissed him on the cheek. "Thank you so very much."

Noah responded, "Abigail, you're like family to me, and soon you will be family. I always wanted to have a son and a daughter. Now my dream will finally come true."

Abigail smiled. "I would feel honored if you considered me your daughter."

"Dad," Christian said, a little confused at how things were playing out before him, "if we're picking out our rings tomorrow, what's in the jewelry box?"

Noah looked down at the red box for a moment, then placed it into his son's hand but didn't let go of it. Father and son looked at each other. "Son, this is my engagement gift for Abigail and you. I will respect and understand if you two decide to turn this gift down." Noah removed his hand and returned to his chair.

"I don't understand, Dad." He looked at the red box, then at Abigail, and finally at his father.

"You will soon. Trust me, son. Now propose to Abigail. You're keeping a very beautiful young lady waiting."

Christian's attention focused anew on Abigail. He stared deep into her eyes. "I love you." He got down onto one knee, then slowly opened the box, not taking his eyes off Abigail. "Will you marry me?"

Abigail's eyes filled with wonderment and awe. Her mouth opened in a silent "ohhhh." She stood speechless. The ring was stunning, more beautiful than she could ever have imagined a ring could be. Abigail's eyes didn't budge from the ring, even when she heard her mother crying. Isabelle buried her head in Ian's chest, muffling the sound of her sobs.

"Dad, why is Mom crying?" Abigail asked, her gaze still locked on the beautiful, sparkling ring.

Ian looked over at Noah. He knew Noah was making the greatest sacrifice he could make for Abigail. "The last time your mother and I saw that ring is the day Christian's mother passed away," Ian told his daughter.

Like sunlight breaking through dark clouds, everything fell into place for Abigail. This was Elizabeth's wedding ring! She turned to Noah, tears falling from her eyes like raindrops in a light April shower. She tried to speak, but no words would come.

"Elizabeth would've been proud and honored to see you wear her ring, your ring now, as would I," Noah said, tender contentment in his voice.

"Then I would be proud and honored to wear it for Elizabeth and you, and also myself. I will wear it every day with pride, reminded of the love you two shared, and still do. The sacrifice you've made to give me this ring, an everlasting symbol of your love for Christian's mom, is so profound to me. I promise you, I will cherish this ring each and every day for the rest of my life, never forgetting or tarnishing the love entrusted to me in this engagement band."

Abigail turned back to Christian, who still waited on bended knee. "Yes! I will marry you!" she said, quaking with excitement.

Christian stood up, took the ring from the box, and slid it onto Abigail's finger.

Abigail smiled, her tear-filled eyes twinkling. "Your mother's ring fits my hand perfectly, like it was meant for my finger!"

"Her ring was meant for your finger," Christian said softly.

Abigail wiped the tears from her eyes. She walked over to Noah and put both of her hands on his cheeks. "You're a good man with an exceptional heart. Thank you so much for making a great night extraordinary."

"You're very welcome."

Christian walked over to his dad and thanked him. Tonight, his dad seemed different, softer perhaps. He had been so private through the years and seldom talked about his wife to anyone. Maybe tonight was a good time to ask him more about her.

"Dad, would you mind telling Abigail and me the story behind the ring? It would mean a great deal to both of us and make us appreciate the ring even more."

Noah cleared his throat. "It's a platinum ring with a one and a half carat princess cut diamond as the main stone. There are six smaller princess diamonds channeled on each side of the main stone, representing the twelve months we courted before I proposed. I worked very hard, putting in many hours of overtime to pay for it. Elizabeth loved it, so to me it was worth every penny."

Abigail looked down at her engagement ring and smiled, then looked back to Noah. "If there is anything I can do for you to show my gratitude for your overwhelming kindnesses, please ask."

"Actually, there is something I would love to have you do for me."

"What is it?"

Noah stared at Abigail's guitar resting silently on the couch. "Would you mind playing that beautiful song again? I would love to hear it just one more time."

Abigail nodded, then went over to the couch, picked up her guitar, and sat down. She cradled the instrument in her arms and started to sing "A Moment Like This" again.

When Abigail finished the last note of the song, Noah grasped the handle of his cane with a firm grip and struggled out of his chair. He felt exhausted and he ached. The long, arduous day had taken a toll on his frail body, and tomorrow wasn't looking any more merciful to Noah.

"I'll be going now. I'm very tired," Noah said.

"Let me walk you to the door." Isabelle stood up and took his arm.

Ian maneuvered himself to Noah's other side and held onto the arm of his old friend. The three proceeded through the house, down the porch steps, and down the cobblestone sidewalk to Noah's car. Ian opened the driver's side door and helped Noah into the seat, with Isabelle's assistance. Once Noah was buckled in, Ian handed him his cane. Noah threw it onto the passenger seat in disgust.

"Do you have any plans for lunch tomorrow, Noah?" Isabelle asked.

Noah looked up at her and nodded his head. "I have an appointment tomorrow morning I need to attend. Can I take a rain check?"

"You sure can."

Noah didn't want to tell his old friends that his doctor had scheduled an appointment at the Mayo Clinic in Rochester the following morning. He was supposed to get the results of his cancer tests to make sure it was still in remission. He was nervous and didn't want to worry them. It would be a two-hour drive each way and God knows how long a wait once he got there.

Noah's bones had been aching all day. His bed was beckoning him to come home to sleep. It was time to go.

"Do you need me to go with you, Noah?" Ian asked.

"No, I think it's better I go it alone."

"Very well then. Isabelle and I are a phone call away if you need us." Ian shut the driver's side door.

Noah started his car and rolled down the window, but he didn't say another word. He just nodded his head in acknowledgement and drove down the driveway and out of sight.

Ian and Isabelle put their arms around one another and walked back up the cobblestone sidewalk to the house. Christian and Abigail were just coming out the front door.

"You two kids have any plans now?" Isabelle asked.

"No, we're just going to sit on the porch swing and talk," Christian replied.

"All right then, enjoy the rest of the evening."

Isabelle and Ian went inside the house and shut the stained glass door behind them.

The old wooden swing had hung from the rafters of the porch overhang for as long as Christian could remember. He and Abigail had spent many long summer evenings in that swing. They had watched many sunsets disappear into darkness on the horizon and had seen the oak trees grow through the passing years.

As they sat down, Christian couldn't take his eyes off the engagement ring. He was captivated. The brilliant, fiery sparkle of the ring when the late evening sunlight kissed the diamonds was as radiant as the sparkle in Abigail's eyes.

"What's on your mind, Christian? Is everything okay?" She looked at him staring at the ring, unable to determine what he was thinking.

Christian looked up into Abigail's eyes. "It's just that I haven't seen many of my mother's personal belongings. The fire destroyed most everything when I was little, and now, being able to look at this ring that was once my mother's on your finger... it's like..." Christian paused for a second, trying to find the right words. "Well, it's like finding a long-lost treasure. It's just amazing."

"I love you," Abigail whispered as she hugged him.

"I love you, too. My birthday is coming up, and I'm going to take you someplace special."

"Hey, no way. I was going to take you out!"

"Don't worry, you still can," he said with a smile. "Just promise me I can have the first hour in the morning."

"I promise," Abigail avowed.

They spent the next hour not saying much, just holding hands and enjoying each other's company. They watched the cardinals and sparrows eat off the bird feeders and listened to them croon their love songs back and forth to one another. They watched the squirrels frolic in the tall oak trees, gathering acorns for the months yet ahead. As the day faded into dusk, Christian leaned over and gave Abigail a long, passionate kiss, a perfect ending to the evening, like a wonderful sentence ending the last chapter of a good story.

"I'll pick you up at nine tomorrow morning. We'll get some breakfast and then head over to see Bear and pick out our wedding rings."

"Okay," Abigail said, getting up and walking to the front door. "Thank you for giving me a wonderful evening I will never forget. I'm so in love with you." She kissed him again and then opened the front door. She hesitated for just a moment, then went inside.

Christian, like a true gentleman, waited on the porch until he heard Abigail lock the door. The porch lights went off afterwards. He stood there alone for a moment, then turned and went down the porch steps into the twilight.

He thought he was on the cusp of something great, just as his dad and mom once were many years before. Christian's feet slid across the cobblestone sidewalk without effort, as if he were gliding on air.

As he jumped into his truck, he looked back at the house one last time. Abigail was standing in her bedroom window, watching him with adoring eyes. She smiled and waved, then drew the blinds closed. Her elegant silhouette disappeared when she turned off her lights. Christian put the truck into gear and rolled down the long driveway, disappearing from sight somewhere between twilight and night.

Chapter 5

SANDS IN THE HOURGLASS

The constant, obnoxious droning of his alarm clock rousted Noah from his peaceful slumber. The time was six in the morning. Grumbling, he reached over and turned off the alarm clock with an angry swat of his hand.

"I hate hospitals and doctors," Noah muttered under his breath. He sat up and turned the bedside lamp on, squinting in the harsh, bright light. Noah sat there for a minute, unsuccessful in his attempts to clear the cobwebs from his drowsy head. He stretched and yawned, trying to get himself motivated for his long day ahead. He slid his feet into his warm, woolen slippers and, with the help of his cane, stood up.

Noah's entire body seemed to throb with pain. He gingerly walked into the bathroom and turned the shower on. Once the water was good and hot, he removed his cozy flannel pajamas, opened the shower curtain, and stepped into the steam, which rolled out like a thick blanket of fog. He eased himself into the piping hot water, which made his skin turn beet red. This was the only way Noah knew of to relieve his tormenting aches and pains, if only temporarily. The heat eased the constant throbbing that penetrated deep down inside his sensitive bones. For Noah, a hot twenty minute shower was like receiving a full, deep-body massage.

Noah shut off the water, reached for his towel, and dried off as fast as his body would allow. He stepped out of the shower, slow and deliberate, careful to reach his cane. He maneuvered himself in front of the mirror, wiping away the steam from the glass with his hand.

"I look like utter hell," he said to himself while gazing at his reflection. He hardly recognized the man in the mirror. Everything in his appearance, plus the way he felt inside, led Noah to believe the stalemate with the cancer was at an end.

He tried not to think about how he looked as he resumed his activities, putting on deodorant and Old Spice cologne, brushing and flossing his teeth, then rinsing with peppermint-flavored mouthwash. He was moving a little bit faster as he returned to the bedroom. The hot shower had dulled his extreme soreness, but Noah knew the throbbing pain would return to torment him soon enough. He looked over to the alarm clock: half past six. He thought he was making outstanding time, considering his condition.

The closet doors flung open, Noah scoured his wardrobe for something that would be comfortable. Yesterday's newspaper forecasted high heat and humidity for today, with a seventy-five percent chance of rain later in the afternoon. Noah picked out a newer pair of khaki pants and navy blue polo shirt. He also grabbed a lightweight jacket to keep him warm inside the Mayo Clinic. The last few times he visited there, the air conditioning chilled him to the bone, making him ache even that much more.

Noah proceeded to the kitchen. He was somewhat hungry but didn't have a lot of time to make anything for breakfast. He spotted an apple left over from baking pies the previous day. "I'll eat this in the car," Noah said to himself as he picked it up. He grabbed a tall bottle of water from the refrigerator, picked up his car keys from the table, and moved toward the door. Beside the door hung a calendar with today's date circled in red: July 1st. Today Noah would meet with Dr. Victor to find out his test results. Noah removed his slippers, put on a pair of brown sandals, and went outside, closing the door behind him.

The morning was glorious, as if God had taken a paintbrush to the canvass we call life and stroked his bold masterpiece. The sky, colored a deep, azure blue, cradled a brilliant sun, which kissed every facet of the earth with its warm rays of light. Birds of every type and size were scattered on the landscape, some on the lush green grass, some flying high in the sky, and some nested in the apple trees surrounding the house.

Noah walked through the gate of the white picket fence to his car, breathing in the morning air, deep and steady as he went. He stopped for a moment, closed his eyes, and took a mental picture of this morning, etching it deep into his memory so he could reflect upon it whenever he became sad or defeated. He was preparing himself for the possibility of darker days ahead.

Noah sat down in the seat of his trusty car, putting the apple and cane on the passenger seat and the water bottle in the cup holder. He buckled up and looked at the clock: a quarter to seven, right on time to make it to the Mayo Clinic by nine, maybe even sooner. As Noah pulled out of the driveway and onto the road, he wasn't aware he was embarking on an impossible journey that would change everything he ever knew about life and death. He was guided along the sometimes-rocky path we call enlightenment.

Independence Day was just a few days away, thus many people were on vacation so traffic was much lighter than usual. Noah's teeth chattered as he ate his apple. His mind raced with an overwhelming feeling of dread as his car sped down the highway. Soon he would find out if the cancer he was battling was still in remission. He drank his water with slow sips. Drinking it too fast would make his knotted stomach hurt much more than it already did.

Noah arrived at a quarter to nine. The two-hour drive felt like an eternity. His body ached and his mind was numb. He took a last sip of water, wiped his lips on his jacket sleeve, then opened the car door, cane in hand. "Here we go," he muttered to himself. Then, one step at a time, he made his way toward his appointment, knowing that with each passing step, he was closer to finding out if the sand in his hourglass was running empty.

* * *

Christian rang the doorbell to Abigail's house shortly before nine. The temperature was rising on this hot, sticky July morning, like bread dough baking in the oven. "I'm glad I wore shorts and a tee shirt," Christian muttered to himself as he waited for Abigail to answer the door. The anticipation of seeing her this morning made him feel like an impatient schoolboy.

The front door swung open, revealing Abigail in all her splendid beauty. She stood in the doorway smiling at Christian, a look of contentment painted upon her young face. She was wearing a red sundress with white daisies printed upon it. On her head, Abigail wore two simple but stylish silver butterfly barrettes, which accented her flowing brown hair. Each barrette held her hair in place and out of her eyes. She walked onto the porch and put her arms around him.

"Good morning, my beautiful fiancé. You look stunning," Christian said, looking in wonderment at the beauty that radiated from her eyes.

"Are you going to ogle me all day or are you going to kiss me?" Abigail asked, teasing him.

"I'm sorry for staring," he replied, pretending to wipe drool from his lips. "I didn't think it was possible to get any hotter out here, and then you emerged. The moment I saw you I just melted. It's hopeless. My heart is irrevocably yours." Christian leaned forward and kissed Abigail on her tender lips.

"Well, aren't you just so sweet," Abigail teased, biting her bottom lip. Christian loved it when Abigail did that with her bottom lip. This was just one of many lighthearted, innocent, cute things she did that drove him crazy with gaiety.

"Are you hungry?" he asked.

"I'm famished."

"Good. I placed an order for us at the greasy spoon in town. Let's hurry and get there before our breakfast gets cold," he said, looking at his wristwatch. Christian put his arm around Abigail and escorted her down the cobblestone sidewalk to his truck. He opened the passenger side door for her and held her hand as she got in.

"Aww, what a gentleman. You're sweet and thoughtful."

She buckled her seatbelt as Christian closed her door and walked around to the driver's side. Abigail's light blue eyes watched him the whole time, her soft gaze fixed on him, never faltering.

Christian sat down inside his cold truck and buckled his seat belt. He thought it had been a darn good idea to leave the truck running with the air conditioner on, since the truck's outside temperature gauge registered eighty-eight degrees.

"Are you excited to pick out your wedding ring, Abigail?" Christian put his truck into gear and started to roll down the driveway.

"Nervous."

"Why are you nervous?"

"It's just…" Abigail paused, searching her heart for the right words to say while reflecting on her engagement ring. "It's just that your mother's ring is so beautiful. I want to find a wedding ring to complement it, not take away from it. Does that make any sense to you?"

"It makes perfect sense to me," Christian said sincerely, which comforted Abigail.

"Thank you," she replied in a quiet yet confidant voice. "I feel a lot better now."

"Look, Abigail. We have a five thousand dollar wedding gift allowance from my dad waiting for us at the jewelry store. I'm sure you'll find something beautiful to go with the engagement ring within our budget. If you want, I have money set aside in savings at the bank we could tap into, but I would prefer not to. I think it would be insulting to my father if we used our own money. He wanted to do this for us for our wedding present. I think we should respect his wishes. Besides, I don't need anything extravagant or flashy, just something simple. Something I can keep on at all times, even during army reserve training. I'm pretty sure I can find a ring that will leave you with most of the money. Is that okay with you?"

Abigail nodded in agreement. "Okay, as long as we pick out your ring first. That way I know how much money I have left to work with."

"Let's eat breakfast and then we'll see what life throws our way." Christian pulled his truck into the parking lot of the diner and parked.

Abigail smiled. "All right then. Let's eat."

* * *

The small examination room was cold and lonely. Noah hated to wait, and he had been fidgeting for almost an hour. The feeling of not being in control of his own destiny made him very uneasy inside, but he could do nothing except stare at the clock on the wall and squirm with impatience. The room was deathly quiet. The only sound that broke the silence was the steady ticking of the second hand of the clock on the wall.

"A quarter to ten," Noah grumbled. He wondered to himself why it was taking so long for Dr. Victor to meet with him. Noah began to pace back and forth, pounding his cane hard onto the floor with each painful step he took.

Finally, a soft knock echoed off the door. In walked Dr. Victor, a tall man with salt-and-pepper hair and a matching mustache. He was roughly the same age as Noah, and possessed a distinguished look about him. Noah noticed many laugh lines around Dr. Victor's eyes, but he also noticed a lot of worry lines etched deep into his forehead. Noah was hoping to see only those laugh lines today.

"Good morning, Mr. Bryson. Would you like to sit down so we can discuss your test results?" Dr. Victor asked. He motioned for Noah to take a seat in the chair.

"I think I will stand. I can't sit still," Noah replied, knots twisting his stomach like a pretzel.

"Very well, Mr. Bryson." Dr. Victor opened up and read from the medical chart in his hands. "After going through all the test results, I am sorry to inform you your cancer is back and has spread aggressively."

"Oh my God!" Noah moaned, his voice barely audible. He moved to the chair and sat down. The look of impending defeat in his eyes was unmistakable. Even though he knew what the answer would be, he asked anyway. "How bad is it?"

"I'm sorry, Mr. Bryson. Your cancer is terminal."

"Checkmate," Noah murmured. He tightened his lips, trying in vain to fend off the tears welling up in his eyes. "How long do I have?"

"In my opinion, one week, possibly two."

Noah closed his eyes as tears rolled down his cheeks, like water cascading down a waterfall. All he could think about was how he would tell Christian and Abigail.

"Once again, I'm very sorry. I wish I could do more." Dr. Victor rested his hand on Noah's shoulder. "Take as much time as you need in here. I'll call your pharmacy and set up a prescription plan to help ease your pain."

Noah's head hung low. He looked at the floor and said nothing. He couldn't muster a single word to tell Dr. Victor he had heard what he just said. He barely managed to nod his head. The doctor left the room, shutting the door behind him.

Noah was alone with his thoughts. The only thing he could hear in the stillness was that clock, that damn second hand relentlessly ticking away toward his date with the inevitable: death. Noah struggled to get on his feet. He gritted his teeth and leaned hard on the walking stick that haunted his soul without respite. "It's time for me to go home," he said to himself, taking a long, slow, deep breath. The walls around him seemed to echo "It's time. It's time."

* * *

Christian and Abigail, sated from a large breakfast, walked into the jewelry store, holding each other's hands. The time: ten o'clock on the nose. They were right on schedule for their appointment with Bear.

"You must be Christian and Abigail," a voice called out from behind the counter. An incredibly tall, muscular man walked out and greeted them. "My name is Theodore, but many of my friends call me Teddy or Bear. You can call me either one."

Christian and Abigail looked at the enormous man standing before them, a gentle giant, a teddy bear. His name fit him very well, since he stood six feet, seven inches tall. He weighed close to three hundred pounds, but he wasn't fat, he was just a solid, well-built man. Bear's hands were enormous, like catchers' mitts, and if you didn't know him, you'd be intimidated in his presence. His voice, however, was soft and gentle, and Abigail and Christian were very comfortable in his company.

"So, let me see the ring, darling," Bear said to Abigail. She extended her arm and Bear took her hand with his big paws. His eyes looked at the ring with a kindness and affection not seen in many men. Bear was a sentimental man, this was easy to tell. "I'm breathless. The ring looks even more amazing on your finger than it did in the jewelry box."

"You've seen the ring before?" Christian asked.

"Last night was the first time I ever laid eyes on it" Bear answered. "It's funny. I've known your dad for close to ten years, Christian. Once, long ago, he told me about losing almost everything he owned in a house fire. Then he comes in here last night, drops this ring on me, and tells me the story of you two wanting to get married. He wanted to give this ring to you both as an engagement gift, and I'm glad to see his wish come true. He really wanted you to wear this ring, Abigail."

Abigail was touched, knowing the sacrifice Christian's dad had made to give her something so special that had once belonged to his beloved wife.

"I'm also supposed to give this to you both," Bear said. He handed Abigail a sealed manila envelope.

"What is this?" she asked.

"It's an appraisal of the ring, a rough one but an appraisal nonetheless. I didn't have much time to get it done, but it's good enough for now. You can submit this to your insurance agent to get temporary coverage. We'll make another, more formal, detailed appraisal after you select your wedding ring, Abigail."

Abigail opened the envelope, wanting but also not wanting to know the ring's value. It didn't matter to her if the appraisal was high or low. The ring possessed so much sentimental value she couldn't fathom putting a price tag on it.

Abigail looked at the appraisal, and her eyes widened. "Oh my Lord, it can't be… sixteen thousand dollars," she whispered in utter disbelief.

Christian's head snapped to attention. "What!"

"Sixteen thousand dollars," Abigail repeated, a little louder this time.

"What!" Christian exclaimed again.

"She said sixteen thousand dollars," Bear said, smiling.

"Holy crap!" Christian said. He couldn't believe what his ears just heard.

"You can say that again," Abigail concurred. She stood there in total shock.

"Look kids, don't look at the ring as money or dollar signs. Look at it as a symbol of Noah's love for you two, because anything less would be a travesty of the amazing gift he has sacrificed for both of you."

Abigail couldn't contain her tears, tears of joy. Bear handed her some tissues and smiled.

"Okay kids. Let's go get some wedding rings picked out."

* * *

Noah spent his long drive home in a silent, mind-numbing purgatory: no radio, no music, nothing. He was suffering from a painful misery that plunged his soul deep down into a dark, cold abyss. Every town he passed on his way back home was a complete blur. He didn't remember any of them. He almost missed his own exit but, luckily, he noticed the turn at the last second and veered onto the exit ramp. Noah would soon be home, back where he belonged.

Out of nowhere, an uncontrollable urge beckoned Noah to his next destination, but it wasn't a voice calling him. This was something else, more like a feeling of clarity, like someone or something guiding him.

It only took a few minutes for Noah to arrive at the cemetery. He parked his car and stepped out, his infernal cane in hand. The heat lingered in the afternoon air, and the unforgiving humidity choked him as he stepped out of his car. Noah felt he had been cast right into the depths of hell. Storm clouds were moving in from the west, and the wind was gathering strength. It wouldn't be long before the dark, grey clouds above would release rain down onto him with all of their might.

Noah limped with tremendous pain through the cemetery until he reached where Elizabeth was buried. He knelt down at the foot of her grave, his head lowered in painful despair. Noah was ready to give up, and when he did, he had to be with her.

"Hello, Elizabeth. I'm sorry I haven't visited in a while. It has just been so hard for me. This cancer is ruthless and methodical, devastating me without remorse. When I look into the mirror, I can't even stand to see the sight of my reflection. I just didn't want you to see me like this."

Noah stretched out on his back next to Elizabeth's grave. Soon he would be able to rest next to her, buried beneath the ground where he was now lying. The never-ending pain would soon end. Soon, however, was not quick enough for him. His eyes were heavy, his mind numb, and his body broken. His empty soul harbored no will to fight this losing battle anymore. Noah closed his eyes and drifted away, surrendering himself to the death that had been stalking him for the past two years.

A delicate orange-and-black Monarch butterfly with white spots on her wings floated quietly past Noah's head and landed by his feet. Noah never saw her. He had drifted too far away from the grace of her love.

* * *

It took Christian a mere ten minutes to find a ring he loved. The style of the ring was simple, yet elegant, and carried no design at all. Just a thick heavy platinum band, exactly what he wanted to wear. It was suitable for his service in the Army National Guard; he wouldn't have to remove it while on duty.

Abigail, however, took over two hours to settle her heart on a ring. The ring she picked was extraordinary. It looked exquisite when placed on her finger next to the engagement ring. The wedding ring she opted for was simple in design but elegant. A platinum ring with six princess cut diamonds set in a channel, which ran across the band.

"I believe we have a winner. Abigail, this wedding ring accents and complements your engagement ring well," Bear said. He was pleased she had found something she loved.

"It's perfect," Abigail said. She purred with delight as she gazed at both rings next to each other.

Both Christian and Abigail thanked Bear for all his time and patience. The two left the jewelry store, holding hands, happy.

"Let's go back to your house and watch a movie," Christian suggested.

"Good idea. I need a little mental break."

"What type of movie are you in the mood for?"

"Can we do a love story… like 'The Notebook?'"

"Abigail, anything you want, I am fine with."

* * *

"Come back to me, Noah, come back. It is not your time yet," said a warm, familiar voice, speaking ever-so-softly to him. This sweet voice, not heard in almost twenty-one years, thawed his icy soul from the frozen talons of death. Noah knew who she was and sat up, rubbing his eyes in disbelief. Standing by his feet was Elizabeth, a soft white glow emanating from her being. Her long brunette hair danced with the wind. She wore a long, white, silk robe, which flowed down to her feet. The robe, held in place at the waist with a white sash, hugged her beautiful curves. Delicately placed on the left side of Elizabeth's head, just above her ear, was a white rose. Only one item of color graced Elizabeth's aura. Located a few inches above her ear, on the right side of her head, was an orange-and-black crystal barrette of a Monarch butterfly, which kissed her flowing brown hair with a stylish, yet resplendent grace.

"Am I dead, Elizabeth?" Noah's voice was cracking. He was unsure if he should be afraid or calm.

"No, Noah. You're not dead."

"Then what am I? Asleep? Awake? What then? I don't understand." A sharp look of bewilderment had cast itself upon his face.

"Let's just say you are someplace in between, my love. You're at the crossroads of your life. You have a bridge to cross but cannot. You still have a toll to pay, a purpose to fulfill."

Noah tried to stand up, desperate in his attempts, but he couldn't rise. The pain was too overwhelming. He needed to hold Elizabeth in his arms, to touch her again. Noah struggled with vehement determination, but it was to no avail. He seemed mysteriously frozen to the ground, and no matter how hard he tried to stand, he could not.

"Soon, my love, soon," Elizabeth said softly in the most soothing, comforting voice imaginable to Noah. "Then you will have all the answers your heart has been longing to know. First, you must take care of some unfinished business. Make sure you settle your affairs, and make sure our son receives the letter I left you. The sands in your hourglass are running out. The time is now upon you for your purpose."

Elizabeth started to drift backwards. She faded from his sight, right before his eyes. Just as she disappeared from him, her voice rang out: "Wake up, Noah!"

At that exact moment, lightning streaked across the grey sky, and the thunder rolled like a freight train through his ears. Noah jumped to his feet. He was now awake and aware of his surroundings. Rain poured down hard onto his body, and washed away all the sorrow and grief his burdened soul had carried. For the first time in a long time, he experienced no pain at all.

"Thank you, Elizabeth!" Noah yelled out to her. He ran to his car, his pace swift to get out of the rain. He left the hated cane that had enslaved his resolve lying on the ground atop his gravesite. For today, the only thing buried at that site would be his cane, and for the rest of Noah's days, his spirit would be confined no more.

Noah jumped into his car and drove home, his purpose clear: to take care of his affairs. He ran into his house and rushed into his office. He opened the safe, removing a black leather attaché case. He left a faded envelope, which had long since turned yellow, inside the safe. For now at least, that letter would remain secure, hidden away.

Noah then rushed back out into the rain and into his car, to make the short drive to Ian and Isabelle's place.

Chapter 6

THE SETTLING OF AFFAIRS

July precipitation is usually warm, but not this afternoon. Today's raindrops were cold and hard like steel, the day raw and bitter. The incoming storm had rolled in quickly. Thunder cracked and lightning streaked across the grey sky. The hail fell next, coming down hard, hammering the rooftops with a steady pounding.

"Wow, that's loud," Ian said as he sat down for coffee with Isabelle at the dining room table. The lights flickered a few times but managed to remain on.

The melodious chime of doorbell rang out through the house. "Who the heck would be out in this weather?" Isabelle asked, going to answer the door.

To her surprise, Noah stood on the porch, soaked from head to toe. "You better get in here before you catch pneumonia," Isabelle said, scolding him as he entered. "Ian is at the dining room table. Get your butt in there and get some hot coffee. I'll be there in a few minutes after I fetch you some dry towels." Isabelle didn't notice Noah was without his cane. She was too busy worrying about getting him warm and dry.

Noah walked into the dining room and sat down, placing his attaché case on the table. Ian closed his newspaper and looked at his friend.

"What brings you over here today, Noah?"

"I'm here for your wife."

Ian raised his left eyebrow, taken aback by Noah's bold statement. "You can't have her. I need her," he teased.

Noah laughed. "I didn't mean it like that. I need her legal expertise. I also need to talk to you."

Isabelle returned to the dining room and handed Noah a few dry towels. Then she poured him a hot cup of coffee and sat down at the table with them both.

"To what do we owe the pleasure of this unexpected visit from you?" Isabelle asked, curious to know why he was out in this weather.

Noah pondered for a moment, flirting with the idea of telling them what had just happened at the cemetery, but he decided against it. That would be his little secret.

"Are Abigail and Christian here?" Noah asked.

"Yes. They're upstairs watching a movie," Isabelle replied. "Do you want me to get them down here?"

"Yes, please."

Isabelle yelled up the stairway for Abigail and Christian to come down and join them. It only took a few seconds for them to reach the dining room.

"Hello, Dad," Christian said, entering the room with Abigail by his side.

Noah motioned for Christian and Abigail to join him at the table with Ian and Isabelle. Noah smiled as he watched Abigail and his son sit down next to each other. They reminded him of himself and Elizabeth so many years before. "Did you get your wedding rings picked out today with Bear?"

"We did, and they're just beautiful," Abigail answered.

"Have you two decided on a wedding date?"

Christian looked at Abigail and smiled. "We're thinking of the fall of next year sometime. Why do you ask?"

Noah looked at each one of them, thinking of all the fond memories they had formed at the antique table through the years. What he was about to tell them would not be among those happy reminiscences.

Noah's eyes moistened with pride and emotion. "I would've loved to see you two get married, but I won't be able to. I learned earlier today my cancer is back, and it's terminal."

Everyone sat silent, their heads lowered as the crushing news pressed onto them with cruelty. No one could speak for several moments. Christian asked the dreaded question, even though he didn't want to hear the answer: "How much time do you have left?"

Tears formed in Noah's beleaguered eyes. "The doctor said one, possibly two more weeks."

An oppressive silence hung in the room, like the calm before a violent storm. Abigail jumped up. To the shock of everyone, she slammed her fist down onto the table, then looked at each of them, resting her final gaze on Noah. "No! I'll be damned if you're going to etch a bad memory into my mind at this table! How dare you!" she scolded, desperate with anger, fear, and grief. Her face turned red, and her eyes burned with an unfamiliar fury.

"Abigail!" Ian's voice echoed through the room with a tremendous thunder. "I'm disappointed you would talk to Noah like that. He's family."

Noah took Abigail's hand, letting her know it was okay, he wasn't upset by her reaction.

Ashamed, Abigail calmed herself and looked to Noah. "I'm sorry, I had no right to speak to you that way. Can you forgive me?"

"I'm the one who should be sorry, Abigail, not you. I just dropped one hell of a bombshell on you all without any warning. It's understandable you would be mad."

Abigail squeezed Noah's hand and turned to her dad and apologized for her actions. "Dad, can I ask you for your help in making this bad memory into a good one?" she asked, a fierce new determination replacing her anger.

Ian could see the wheels turning in his daughter's mind through her sparkling blue eyes. He knew all too well she had an idea brewing in her pretty little head.

"What do you suggest, Abigail?"

Abigail pleaded, a hint of desperation in her soft voice. "Dad, please marry Christian and me this week. Marry us in the little chapel in the back of our church."

"Slow down, Abigail," Isabelle said. "If your dad marries the two of you, he won't be able to walk you down the aisle and give you away."

Abigail looked at her dad, knowing his dream was always to give his only daughter away when she married. "Dad, if Noah can't see his very own son marry me, I'll regret it for the rest of my life, and I know you will, too."

Ian knew his daughter's words were true. He would regret it if Noah didn't get to see Christian and Abigail get married. Ian knew he had to honor his daughter's request, to make this sacrifice for her.

"Okay, I'll marry you and Christian on Saturday, July 5th at one in the afternoon. That's four days from now."

"Thank you, Dad. I appreciate it." A big grin now covered Abigail's face from ear to ear as she let out a loud sigh of relief.

She then turned her attention to Noah. "Will you do the honor of walking me down the aisle and giving me away to your son?"

Noah looked over to Ian, not wanting to say yes without his approval. Abigail was his daughter, after all. Ian nodded, and Noah refocused his attention on Abigail. "I would be honored to walk you down the aisle."

Abigail turned to Isabelle. "Mom, will you please be my matron of honor?"

Isabelle couldn't speak. She was sobbing too hard. All she could do was nod her head to Abigail.

"I'll ask Alexander to serve as my best man when he gets back home," Christian said.

Abigail sat back down in her chair. "It's settled, then."

"Speaking of settling things, I have some business to conduct with you all," Noah said. He opened his attaché case and removed some documents. "This is my will. Would you please review it again and verify everything is in proper order, Isabelle?" He slid the stack of documents across the table to her.

"Of course," Isabelle agreed, but she knew it would feel strange to look at Noah's will. The finality of the situation shook Isabelle to the core. The loss of Elizabeth was hard enough, and losing Noah would be just as devastating.

Noah stood up from the table without effort and pushed in his chair. "I think I'll be going now. I'm exhausted and have a date with my bed."

"Dad, where in the world is your cane?" Christian asked, watching his dad stand with ease.

"Don't need it anymore. It slows me down!" Noah winked and flashed a toothy smile to everyone. He turned and walked out as if he were floating on cloud nine.

None of them could believe their eyes. Noah had been struggling, helpless even, without his cane for a long time. His newfound strength stupefied them, and everyone seated at the table could say nothing at all.

* * *

The next three days flew by. Everyone was preparing for the upcoming wedding with the utmost diligence, and sadly, everyone was also readying themselves for a funeral that loomed in the near future.

Isabelle and Abigail worked on the wedding dress. Abigail would be wearing the same gown her mother wore many years before.

Ian prepared for the wedding of his daughter with joy, but in private he prepared a eulogy and made funeral arrangements for his good friend.

Alexander prepared his wedding gift for his sister in secret, with Christian's covert assistance. Alexander had to work fast to contact the people he needed to help pull off his plan.

Christian and Noah spent time alone together. One morning they went fishing, and even though they didn't catch anything, they enjoyed their time together.

Noah's soul was nearing harmony as he settled his affairs. He only had a few more things left to do: the wedding, Elizabeth's old letter in the safe, and saying goodbye. Then, he wouldn't have to fight anymore. He could rest in peace.

Chapter 7

YESTERDAY, TODAY, TOMORROW

Independence Day, Christian's twenty-first birthday, a bittersweet day that had always passed slowly, dragging on like a snail running a race against a turtle. In recent years, Christian had often spent the day alone. This birthday, however, would be different, because Abigail would be joining him for his special day. For Christian, it was time to stop dwelling in the emptiness of yesterday, time to start living in the promises of today, and time to believe unconditionally in the dreams of tomorrow.

Today was an incredible, tranquil morning, not a single cloud sullied the sky, just an unending, vast expanse of blue as far as the eye could see. The stuffy humidity that had choked the air over the past few days had all but abated.

The flourishing lawn on the grounds of the cemetery was always lush and green at the beginning of July when Christian visited his mom's grave. The grass clippings of the fresh cut lawn filled the air with the sweet smell of summer. An enormous patch of wild milkweeds growing beside the cemetery was home to the Monarch butterflies Christian had always seen floating throughout this hallowed ground. Christian didn't think of the cemetery as a place of death. In his heart, he knew it was a sacred place full of life, and seeing the butterflies always reinforced his belief.

Christian walked up to his mother's grave with Abigail right by his side. She carried a dozen long-stemmed snowy-white roses, accented with just a little bit of baby's breath. The rose blossoms were just beginning to open, and their sweet scent escaped into the world. Their scent had penetrated the upholstery of Christian's truck during the drive over to the cemetery, leaving his vehicle smelling like a rose garden.

The day had just begun and the sun was still cresting over the eastern horizon. Christian knew his dad would come here soon, perhaps in an hour or two. His dad would spend the whole day sitting by his mom's grave, just talking or reading a book to her. That's why Christian always came early, to get a little bit of alone time with her on his birthday. But today was different. Today Christian had his one true love by his side.

Abigail leaned down and placed the roses in the flower holder at the foot of the grave. She then stepped back, respectful to give Christian a moment alone with his mom.

"Hello, Mom. I wanted you to see Abigail and me together before we are married tomorrow. I wanted you to see how happy we both are." Christian stood there for a moment and then took Abigail's hand, and pulled her up beside him.

"I will love, treasure, and cherish your son as long as I live. This I promise you," Abigail said softly. Her voice carried a quiet confidence and grace.

Christian looked to Abigail, fondness filling his eyes. Then he looked back at his mother's grave and spoke, "I hope…" He stopped himself, collected his thoughts and started again. "We hope you approve of us getting married, and we also pray for your blessing."

As the last word rolled off Christian's tongue, something beautiful and unexpected happened: a small Monarch butterfly fluttered around them and landed atop one of the white roses. The delicate, fragile wings appeared as if they were hand painted by God himself. The soft, warm, inviting orange color resembled the tint of the setting sun bleeding across the western horizon, and the jet-black trim around the wings' edges matched the ebony keys on a brand new piano. The pristine white spots daubed all over the butterfly's wings were the finishing touches to God's intricate masterpiece.

Abigail turned to Christian, her eyes glistening with awe. "Christian, I'm going to take this butterfly as a symbol of your mother's approval of us getting married. I'm going to hold onto this memory forever. To me, this moment was intimate and personal, and absolutely perfect."

Christian nodded in agreement. "I was thinking the same thing myself."

A few feet away from the foot of Elizabeth's grave was a faded park bench Noah had paid to have placed there soon after Elizabeth passed away. Christian knew his dad would sit on it for hours and talk to his mother. This spot was quite a private place, and Christian understood why his dad would stay for so long on his visits.

Christian asked Abigail to sit with him on the bench. He wanted to share his feelings with her, and they maneuvered themselves to face each other while they conversed.

"Abigail, do you believe things happen for a reason or purpose in life?"

"Yes, I do. I believe we all have certain paths in life to follow. When someone or something presents us with a choice, we forever alter our paths by the direction we choose, like taking one fork in the road rather than the other. We must make our choices with care, because we may never be able to go back and choose the other fork."

Christian sat and pondered what Abigail said. It made a lot of sense to him. He was determined to make the correct choices from here on out for Abigail, and himself.

"Christian," Abigail said softly, trying hard to not intrude. "Would you like to have children of your own some day? If so, when?"

Christian loved children very much. He always tried to volunteer at church for anything kid-related. He detested being an only child. He wished he had a brother or sister, even longed for it. Children of his own, this was something he wanted, sometime soon, quite possibly in the immediate future.

"I'd love to have children with you, Abigail. At least two: one boy and one girl. The boy would carry on the Bryson family name and keep my family's legacy intact. The girl would be my darling little angel."

Abigail grinned. "I'd love to have one boy and one girl too." She was relieved he wanted to have children. "When would you like to start trying for them?"

"We can start soon, right after our wedding if you wish." He brushed her delicate brown hair away from her face and looked into her sparkling light blue eyes.

"Do you promise?"

Christian knew how much she wanted to have children. He also knew she would be an excellent mother. Christian pointed to the roses on his mother's grave with confidence and vowed: "As sure as this Monarch butterfly sitting on this snowy-white rose is my witness, I promise to make you a mom someday soon. I'll try very hard to get you at least one boy and one girl."

Abigail grabbed him and squeezed him so hard he couldn't breathe.

"Am I interrupting anything?" a voice asked from behind the wooden bench.

Christian and Abigail hadn't heard Noah's car pull into the cemetery, and he had managed to walk up behind them, giving them quite a start.

"Dad, you surprised us. You're here much earlier than I expected."

"It's okay," Noah replied to his son. "I didn't have much happening this morning so I decided to come a little earlier than usual and spend some time alone with you before you left."

"Would you like me to leave?" Abigail asked, afraid her presence might upset Noah.

"Oh heavens no, Abigail. I didn't know Christian would bring you here today. You're family now and you're always more than welcome to sit here with us," Noah said, his voice reassuring.

Noah walked around the bench and sat down between Abigail and Christian, putting an arm around each of them. The Monarch butterfly resting on the white rose caught Noah's eye.

"Your mother loved butterflies, Christian. She also loved getting roses."

The three of them sat in silence, reflecting on the picture-perfect image in front of them until the butterfly lifted into the air and gracefully fluttered away to the milkweed patch.

Soon after, Christian and Abigail rose. It was Abigail's turn to take Christian out to paint the town, and she had decided to take him to the Fourth of July festivities. The parade would be starting soon and they needed to hurry to get a good parking spot.

As they walked to his truck to leave, Christian looked back at his dad seated on the bench. He knew deep down inside this would be the last birthday his dad would be alive. Even though he wasn't using his cane any more, Noah looked terrible. A sick feeling swept through Christian's stomach. He knew it wouldn't be long before he would be parentless.

Chapter 8

FIREWORKS AND DREAMS

The parade was the medicine Christian needed to lift his spirits. Floats, clowns, horses, and marching bands excited all during the three-hour extravaganza.

After the parade, Abigail and Christian decided to pig out on carnival food. Street venders were scattered all around town, serving anything you could imagine on a stick. The two of them shared everything: pronto pups, mini donuts, cheese curds, nachos, and cotton candy. The list of delicious food was endless. All anyone needed was a lot of money and a hearty appetite. Christian and Abigail possessed both.

Abigail let out a deep, thunderous belch.

Christian chuckled at her. "Impressive!"

"I'm stuffed," Abigail announced. She rubbed her little tummy and smiled.

Christian looked at Abigail in utter amazement. "You ate way more than me. Where do you put it all?"

"I have a hollow leg!" Abigail wisecracked. She pointed down to her skinny legs and winked.

Christian and Abigail next decided to test their luck at the American Legion bingo tent. They played bingo for a few hours and talked the whole time about their future aspirations. Even though they didn't win anything, they enjoyed each other's company. On the way out of the bingo tent, Christian spotted a pull-tab booth.

"Care to try your luck, Abigail?"

"Oh yeah, I love pull-tabs," she exclaimed, clapping her hands in delight.

Christian took out his wallet and placed a twenty dollar bill on the counter. "I'll take twenty lucky diamonds, please," he said to the woman selling the pull-tabs.

After receiving the tabs, he walked over to Abigail and split them up. "Ten for me and ten for you."

"Thank you," she said.

Christian pulled open all of his tabs, one after the other in rapid succession. "Nothing!" he grumbled. "What about you, Abigail. Any luck?"

"What do all these red lines through the symbols mean?" Abigail asked, biting her lip, aware she had won something big.

"It means you got a winner of some type. What are the symbols?"

"All of them are diamonds," she said with a wink.

"You won five hundred!" Christian said, giving her a congratulatory hug.

Abigail hugged him back. "You're wrong, Christian. *We* won five hundred."

Christian cashed in the winning pull-tab, tipped the girl behind the counter, then split the money with Abigail.

"Here's two hundred and thirty-five for you and two hundred thirty-five for me. Say, these winnings almost cover my losses from all the food you ate earlier."

"Hey now, that's not nice. You are so naughty!" She slugged him hard on his arm.

For being a petite young woman, she could throw a mean left hook, just like a champion prizefighter, Christian thought to himself.

They decided to head down to the beach-front carnival. A vast assortment of rides and midway games were scattered throughout the grounds.

"Hey, let's do the Ferris wheel," Abigail said. She pointed to it and smiled.

"Okay, that'll be fun."

As they got off the Ferris wheel after their ride was over, Christian spotted a little girl. She was alone and crying, standing by the guardrail that encircled the ride. She had red hair and freckles and couldn't be much older than four. Christian walked over and knelt down beside her.

"Are you lost, sweetheart?"

"No, I ran away from my mommy."

Christian looked over to Abigail, who was keeping an eye out for the little girl's mother. He turned back to the little girl.

"What is your name, sweetheart?"

"My name is Eilir Iseult Beddau."

"Well, Eilir, why did you run away?"

"Because I wanted to ride the Ferris wheel, but my mommy has no money to take me."

"Eilir!" a woman called out from the crowd as she spotted her daughter. She raced over and picked the little girl up, trembling with fear. "You scared Mommy. I thought I'd lost you," the woman said with a distinct, but pleasing foreign accent.

Christian stood up and introduced himself and Abigail.

"My name is Eirwen Rhosyn Beddau," the woman said. She thanked Abigail and Christian for watching over her daughter.

Eilir was the spitting image of her mother. Eirwen was a tall, slender, beautiful woman in her mid-twenties. Her long, flowing hair was much like Abigail's, except it was tawny-red.

"You two have beautiful names, and I noticed your foreign accent. Are you from around here?" Abigail asked.

"My husband and I moved here five years ago after my parents died. We're both of Welsh decent."

Christian nodded. "Is your husband around? We'd like to meet him."

"My husband left me soon after Eilir was born. He abandoned us and went back overseas."

"I'm sorry," Abigail said.

"Well, I'm sorry to have interrupted your day. Thank you so much for finding my daughter for me. If there is anything I can do to show my gratitude, let me know."

"Actually, there is something you could do for me," Christian said. "Let me take Eilir on the Ferris wheel."

"Mommy, Mommy, can I go? Please?" Eilir begged. Her eyes were lit up like the Christmas tree in Rockefeller Plaza.

Eirwen was unsure what to say to Christian. She stood there for a moment, holding Eilir and thinking of what she should do. Eirwen was a proud, independent woman who didn't like to depend on others for help. However, in Eilir's short life, she hadn't had much of anything. Eirwen swallowed her pride for the benefit of her daughter. "Yes, you can take her on the Ferris wheel."

Eilir was ecstatic. She climbed down from her mother's arms and grabbed Christian by the hand, dragging him to the entrance of the ride.

Tears started to well up in Eirwen's eyes at the sight of her daughter with Christian.

"Is everything okay, Eirwen?" Abigail asked. She dug into her purse and retrieved some tissues for Eirwen.

"Eilir doesn't know what it's like to have a dad or any male figure in her life for that matter. It just breaks my heart to see them together. Eilir's dad should be here doing what Christian is doing."

After the ride, Christian and Eilir returned to find Abigail and Eirwen giggling together at the sight of Eilir dragging Christian around by the hand as if he were a rag doll.

"Thank you, Christian, for taking Eilir on the Ferris wheel. She hasn't had fun like that before, ever."

"Well then, why should we stop?"

"What do you mean?" Eirwen asked, somewhat confused.

"Eirwen, do you know you have a very intelligent little girl on your hands? She is very smart indeed. Listen, I might be overstepping my bounds here, but Eilir told me you lost your job, and since her dad isn't around, it's been rather difficult to show her a good time."

"What are you trying to say?"

"What I am trying to say is this. Let Abigail and me treat you and Eilir to a time you will never forget. Our treat, no strings attached, for the rest of the evening."

"I don't know what to say."

"Just say yes," Abigail said, smiling.

"Yes, then. Thank you both very much!" Eirwen started to cry again.

"No more crying though, Eirwen," Abigail scolded playfully. "I don't have many tissues left. Now let's go have some fun."

The next several hours went flying by. Eilir managed to drag Christian onto every ride she was tall enough for, at least three times on each. She also won a medium-sized brown teddy bear, which she affectionately named Christian. Abigail and Eirwen talked a lot. During that stretch of time, they built a foundation for what could be a great friendship.

Darkness was settling in, the time nearing half past eight. Christian bought them all ice cream cones and they moved to a picnic table by the beach, where the idle chitchat continued. Abigail learned Eirwen was a legal secretary but she couldn't find a job.

Abigail dug into her purse and pulled out a pen and a sheet of paper. "What's your phone number?" Abigail asked Eirwen. "My mother is looking for a secretary. She runs a law firm that specializes in wills and estates. She wanted me to work the rest of the summer for her, but I think I just found a more qualified candidate. I'll give her your name and number tomorrow, and she'll probably call you on Monday to set up an interview."

"Are you for real?" Eirwen exclaimed, disbelieving what she was hearing. The thought of having a job again to support her daughter lifted her spirits high. "I feel very indebted to you both. If there is any small thing I can do to return the favor, you must tell me."

"There is something you can do, but first I need to check with Abigail. Excuse us one moment," Christian said.

He pulled Abigail aside and whispered into her ear for a few seconds. Abigail's eyes sparkled, and she nodded her head and gave him a hug. The two rejoined Eirwen and Eilir at the picnic table.

Christian smiled. "Eirwen, does Eilir have a pretty little white dress?"

"It's long and white and pretty and lacy!" Eilir said, interrupting her mom before she could even answer.

"Yes, she does," Eirwen said, reconfirming what Eilir had blurted out. "But why do you ask?"

"All in good time, Eirwen, all in good time," Christian said.

Confused, Eirwen looked to Abigail but she just shrugged her shoulders and smiled.

"Abigail, do you still have your pretty silver tiara at home?" Christian asked.

"Yes I do, my love. It's in my jewelry box."

Christian turned to Eilir. He got down onto his knees and looked into her innocent green eyes. "Do you remember telling me during our first ride on the Ferris wheel how you wanted to look like a princess?"

Eilir nodded. "Uh huh, I want to wear a crown and dress like a princess."

"You know what, Eilir? Abigail is going to become my queen tomorrow, and my future queen needs a beautiful princess to assist her. Would you like to serve as Abigail's princess?"

Eilir nodded her head again, this time much more vigorously. She could barely contain her enthusiasm and squealed in delight.

Christian, who was still down on his knees, looked to Eirwen and cleared his throat. "Abigail and I are getting married tomorrow. We respectfully request your presence at noon so your daughter can be our ring bearer and flower girl, all in one."

Eirwen put her hands up to her face, in shock at the invitation for her daughter to participate in their wedding.

"Things happen for a reason, Eirwen," Abigail said. She wrote directions to the church on a piece of scrap paper and told Eirwen, "Make sure to arrive at noon. The ceremony will start at one."

Christian shared with Eirwen the reason he and Abigail had moved up their wedding date: his dad's terminal cancer. He told her how his mother died after childbirth and discussed growing up with only one parent.

Christian and Abigail's story touched Eirwen, so she agreed to let Eilir be their ring bearer and flower girl the following day.

Dusk was settling in. Soon fireworks would fill the night sky with all their brilliant and dazzling colors. The sky seemed like a blank canvas, waiting for an artist to paint a stunning masterpiece on it. They all were sitting right up near the lake and had front-row seats, like being at the circus, waiting for *The Greatest Show on Earth* to begin. The night seemed perfect. Temperatures hovered in the high sixties, no wind, no humidity and, most important, no ravenous blood-sucking mosquitoes.

Abigail nestled up to Christian when the first of the fireworks exploded high in the night sky. Dazzling illumination by spectacular chrysanthemum and peony-shaped explosions filled their eyes with brilliant lights. Their ears filled with crackling sounds that would impress even the harshest critic. Gold, silver, red, orange, blue, green, yellow, purple, every color imaginable awed kids and adults alike during twenty minutes of magnificent splendor. This was Eilir's first fireworks display, and she loved every minute of it. With every breathtaking explosion, she clapped her hands and squealed in sheer delight.

Gradually, the lights and pageantry blurred around Christian, and the sounds faded. His mind drifted to Eilir. Christian couldn't fathom how any father could abandon his child. Eilir may not have been his daughter, but her sweet innocence helped reinforce in him what he wanted the most: children with Abigail.

As the crescendo of the final fireworks exploded deep into the night, the thin haze of smoke cleared, once again revealing the moon and stars in their infinite light. The smell of sulfur lingered for a moment in the cool night air.

Eirwen and Eilir turned toward Christian and Abigail, thanking them again for the superb day they had together, and for a miraculous night. Eilir hugged Christian with all her might, her little arms squeezing as hard as they could around his neck. She didn't want this evening to end, nor did she want to let Christian go.

"It's time to go home now, Eilir," Eirwen said. She rubbed her daughter's back with a gentle love only a mother could give.

"I'll see you tomorrow, Eilir," Christian stated. "I'm looking forward to seeing a beautiful princess."

Eilir loosened her stranglehold on Christian's neck, and leaned back away from him as he held her. She put her dainty little hands on his face, one on each cheek, and said, "I wish you were my daddy." She looked at Christian with all of her child-like innocence and smiled, then kissed him on the forehead.

Christian stood speechless for a moment, amazed at how easy it had been for Eilir to attach herself to him. Happy tears fell from Eirwen's eyes. She knew her daughter had just experienced one of the greatest evenings in her short life.

"If I ever have a daughter, I hope she's just like you." Christian handed Eilir to Eirwen. "Be at the church at noon. We would like to start at one," Christian reminded them.

Eirwen nodded, signaling she understood, then turned and walked away. Eirwen and Eilir slipped away into the crowd and disappeared from Christian and Abigail's sight.

Abigail took Christian's hand and squeezed it. "You're going to make a great daddy one day."

Christian smiled, his soul warmed by Abigail's strong faith in him. She knew how to say all the right words at just the right time. How could he not want to have children with her? She was everything he ever wanted in a woman, and more.

"Would you like to take a moonlit stroll on the beach, birthday boy?" Abigail asked, biting her lower lip.

Christian didn't know how he could say no. She was just so damn cute when she did that.

The two young lovers walked the beach, hand in hand, for the next hour. They talked of their future and dreams together, planning everything out from children to retirement. Christian and Abigail didn't want to stay out too late. After all, they were getting married the next day.

They made it to Abigail's place shortly after eleven o'clock. Abigail stood on the top porch step, while Christian was one step below her. He was still taller, but not by too much now. They were almost at eye level with each other and Abigail liked not having to lean her head back to look into his eyes.

"Thank you for an astonishing day. Thank you for opening yourself up to me. You let me into your heart when we visited your mom, further than I ever thought imaginable," Abigail said, hugging Christian tight. "What you did for Eilir today was extraordinarily selfless. You filled that little girl's heart with joy. To watch Eilir fall for you the same way I did, it was breathtaking."

"You weren't so bad yourself. The way you helped Eirwen out tonight was equally awe-inspiring. Tonight you showed me the sweetness and depths of your never-ending grace."

Christian held Abigail in his arms for quite awhile longer on the porch steps. He loved feeling her heart pounding against his chest, beating steady and true. The crickets made the only sound in the late night air, chirping their love song to one another.

"I think I should get up to bed now, Christian. We both have a long day ahead of us tomorrow." She started to pull away from him, but he couldn't relinquish his grasp of her, not just yet.

"Five minutes more. Please, Abigail," Christian begged, pulling her back into his chest, his plea tender, and sweet. He held her tight, kissing her on her soft lips.

"Okay, five minutes more then, and only five minutes." Her tone was loving, but firm. She squeezed her arms back around Christian, much tighter than she did before. "You have to leave before midnight though, mister. Otherwise, it will be bad luck to see your bride before the ceremony on your wedding day," Abigail playfully scolded.

When it came time for Christian to leave, he let her go, but with reluctance, from his arms. Abigail kissed him one last time, then slipped inside the house, vanishing from him once again.

"Only one long night more, that's all I have to wait." Christian sighed to himself as he left. It might as well have been an eternity. Having to wait to hold her just killed him inside. One more lonely night and Abigail would be his wife. Then he would get to hold her in his arms, all night long, never having to let her go.

Chapter 9

THE SPECIAL MESSAGE

To the east, the morning sun was emerging on the horizon. To the west, the moon was disappearing from sight, much like a person sinking in quicksand. The clear, star-filled sky of the night before had given way to rain clouds, just starting to form off in the distance.

Abigail had just logged off the Internet. She had been doing some light research on genealogy and had also checked on the weather forecast for the day. Downstairs, she found her parents and twin brother sitting at the dining room table having breakfast. "It's going to rain on my wedding day, curse the luck!" Abigail said as she joined them for breakfast.

Her father put down his cup of coffee and looked at his daughter with eyes that reflected the inner beauty of his soul. Ian flashed a peaceful smile her way as he spoke. "You know, Abigail, some people believe rain on their wedding day portends good luck. Others believe angels in heaven are weeping tears of joy for you."

"Thanks, Dad. I feel a lot better now." A gentle calm eased her soul. Her dad always knew how to say the wonderful words to make everything seem more than okay.

Abigail could always see the fortitude her father possessed during his weekly sermons at church. Ian seemed like he could transform lead to gold with merely his voice. His aura was like a lighthouse beacon in the dark night, guiding his congregation, like sailors lost at sea, home to safety.

"You're welcome," Ian replied to his daughter. He smiled and resumed sipping his piping-hot coffee.

"I'm out the door," Alexander mumbled while stuffing his already-full mouth with another bite of eggs.

"Where are you off to?" Isabelle asked.

"It's a surprise. Just don't come to the church before noon," Alexander mumbled again, his mouth still stuffed with his mom's delectable breakfast. He kissed his mother on the cheek and rushed out the door.

"I wonder what he is up to," Abigail said.

Isabelle shrugged her shoulders. "Heaven only knows with that boy."

"Mom and Dad, can I talk to you about something I feel is a specific message from above?"

Intrigued, Ian set his cup of coffee down and focused his attention on his daughter seated across from him.

"You can talk to us about anything," Isabelle said. She took a seat next to her daughter and held her hand in reassurance.

"Okay. I don't want to seem crazy or anything, but something very special happened to Christian and myself yesterday, and I don't believe it was just mere coincidence, either."

"Then what do you believe it was, Abigail?" Ian asked, his voice, calm and steady.

"Christian invited me for the first time to go with him to visit his mother's grave. I brought her a dozen roses."

"Do you mind telling me what color roses?" Isabelle asked.

"They were white."

"White roses. Those were Elizabeth's favorite," Isabelle said as she looked over to her husband. "Please continue, Abigail."

"Shortly after placing the roses into the graveside holder, a butterfly landed on top of them."

Ian perked up; he looked at his wife, then his daughter. "What type of butterfly, Abigail?" he asked.

"A Monarch butterfly."

"Good heavens," Isabelle said, looking at Ian in disbelief.

Ian paused for a moment, thinking of how to respond, then looked into Abigail's eyes. "You're right. This is a very special story, Abigail. You should look at it as a message, a message that Elizabeth is happy for the two of you and..."

"But, Dad, there's more," Abigail interrupted.

"Okay then, go on."

"Later in the day, Christian and I met a young woman and her four-year-old daughter. They were of Welsh descent. I don't think this was a chance meeting."

"I don't understand, Abigail. How so?" her mother asked.

"Mom, this woman was laid off from her job; she is a legal secretary looking for work. I figured you could give her an interview for your law firm. I know you wanted me to fill that job, but I think this woman is destined for it."

"Abigail, I think you might be stretching this destiny thing a bit. But I trust your judgment and I'll give her an interview if you want me to."

"Damn it, Mom, let me finish! This woman's parents are both dead, and the father of her daughter abandoned them and pays no child support. She's all on her own and needs our help."

"Abigail, slow down!" Ian said. "I know you have a good heart and want to help this woman, but I see no reason to think she and her daughter are part of a bigger message."

"Dad and Mom, you still don't understand. The message is in their names. The mother's full name is Eirwen Rhosyn Beddau, and the daughter's is Eilir Iseult Beddau. I looked up the Welsh name meanings on the Internet this morning. Do you have any idea what their names mean?" Abigail quaked with excitement, ready to explode like a shaken can of soda.

Ian and Isabelle shook their heads, but their anticipation had increased, building rapidly as they listened to their daughter speak.

"The mother's first name means snowy white, the middle name means roses, and the last can be translated as from the grave. I put snow-white roses on Christian's mother's grave," Abigail explained. "The daughter's first name means butterfly, the middle name means princess, and the last name again means from the grave. Princess equals royalty, which also translates to monarchy, which is where we get Monarch butterfly."

Flabbergasted, Ian and Isabelle's jaws dropped. Ian looked deep into his wife eyes, the memory of twenty-one years earlier still fresh in his mind. Could this be the purpose foreshadowed to him by Elizabeth in the hospital bed on that day long ago?

"Ian, we need to help this mother and daughter any way we can," Isabelle said.

"Yes, I believe you are right. We do need to help. This to me is a special message we must pursue," he said.

"Abigail, when do we get to meet this Eirwen and Eilir?" Isabelle asked.

"Today! Christian asked Eilir to serve as our flower girl and ring bearer for our wedding."

"Well then, everything should turn out even more joyous than we had expected, even if it does happen to rain," Ian proclaimed.

* * *

In secrecy, Christian and Noah joined Alexander at the church. The three of them would decorate the small chapel usually reserved for intimate affairs, such as baptisms and small weddings. Alexander knew what his sister would want, and he had the help of Christian and Noah at his complete disposal.

The small chapel had a main center aisle that led up to the altar and three rows of pews on each side. A large, ornate, stained-glass window, located behind the altar, arched on the outer wall with grandeur, letting through a natural light that illuminated the room in a soft, colored glow. Overhead, a round skylight focused the sun's light onto the altar, and a baby grand piano hugged the left corner of the room. This little chapel was the most personal, intimate, and private room to celebrate a marriage with close friends and family.

The three men absorbed the ambiance inside the chapel, knowing if they used care and patience in their endeavors to decorate, Abigail would melt just like butter. They had everything they needed to transform the chapel into an idyllic, picturesque masterpiece. Christian and Alexander would place one hundred candles throughout the room. Noah's job would be to pick the petals off the roses and place them throughout the chapel, the only exception being the main center aisle.

"Alright then, let's get started, boys," Noah said, sitting down. He started to pluck the petals off the first rose.

* * *

Abigail and her mother had worked hard all week long on the wedding dress. Isabelle's old dress was just as beautiful as it had been twenty-five years ago. The gown was white and lacy, with small silver sequins throughout that accented the dress much like silver-white stars in the midnight sky.

Abigail's veil was long and would flow over her head and down to her breast, kissing her face with elegance as it covered her.

"Are you excited to wear the dress?" Isabelle asked her daughter. They both stood in Abigail's bedroom, admiring their exquisite work.

Abigail didn't answer her mom. Instead, she rushed into her mother's arms and hugged her tight. "What's the matter, Abigail? Are you nervous?"

"No, Mom. I'm not nervous or scared," she replied, still holding onto her mom. Abigail was ready for marriage with Christian. She had dreamed of this moment ever since she received her first doll when she was a little girl. "I just want to say thank you for everything: this dress, the time we spent altering it, and the twenty plus years of my life. You were always there, being my mother and mentor no matter what."

Isabelle hugged her daughter tight. She felt thankful she'd had the opportunity to raise her child, unlike Elizabeth. She tried to imagine what kind of relationship Christian might have had with his mother. It made Isabelle sad to think of Elizabeth. She wished her old best friend could be here today to watch her son marry Abigail. Isabelle believed Elizabeth would be there in spirit, and Christian was a part of her soul, living proof her legacy carried on.

"Abigail, let's go outside and pick some roses for Eilir's flower basket before it starts to rain. Eilir will need some beautiful rose petals to toss onto the aisle."

Outside in the flower garden, Abigail looked at the array of colors and turned to her mother." Can we just pick white roses?"

"It's your wedding, dear. Just let me know what you want to do."

"Then white roses it is. I believe Christian's mother would've loved that."

"That she would, Abigail. It's a sweet gesture by you to think of her."

The two chatted for a bit as they picked the white roses. Isabelle looked at her watch. "It's starting to get late, Abigail. I think we'd better get inside and eat a light brunch, then get cleaned up and do our makeup. We can put our dresses on at the church in the dressing room."

Abigail nodded.

After eating with Ian, both women went upstairs to wash up and do their makeup. After a while, Ian called upstairs to let them know he would see them at the church as he was leaving to make final preparations for the wedding ceremony. Both Abigail and Isabelle were almost ready to go, just five minutes more.

Outside, the sky was growing ever darker. Large ominous-grey storm clouds loomed overhead. Soon it would be raining. Isabelle and Abigail raced to the car and headed to church, and just in time. No more than one minute after they entered the church lobby, the heavens opened up, and the joyous tears of angels started to rain down on all below.

Chapter 10

INTIMATE AFFAIRS

Eirwen and Eilir waited in the church lobby. They had arrived not much more than one minute before Abigail and her mother. Eilir looked precious in her fluffy white dress, just like a princess.

"I have something for you, Eilir," Abigail said. She knelt down in front of Eilir and showed her the jeweled crown. Eilir was star struck by the shiny-silver tiara; it was sparking and beautiful. Abigail placed the tiara on Eilir's head, and her thick red hair held it in place. Abigail stood up and for a moment admired how cute Eilir looked.

Abigail made the introductions. "Mom, this is Eilir and her mother Eirwen."

"Nice to meet you both. My name is Isabelle. I've heard a lot about you two. Eirwen, we'll talk after the ceremony about setting up a job interview, if that's okay with you."

"That would be great."

Ian rushed out of his office and into the lobby, introducing himself with haste to Eirwen and Eilir. He appeared concerned and flustered, his brow furrowed tight.

"Is everything okay, Dad?" Abigail asked, fretful to hear his reply.

"We have a big problem. The pianist is out ill with the flu. She can't even get out of bed."

Abigail panicked. There would be no music for her wedding! All her dreams were starting to unravel right before her eyes, like a ball of yarn unwound by a mischievous, playful kitten.

"Maybe I can be of help, Abigail," Eirwen said, her voice timid. "My mother taught me to play the piano for many years growing up, but I've never played in front of an audience. If you trust me, I'll give it my best shot because of all you have done for Eilir and me."

Abigail looked at Eirwen. Everything thus far had happened for a reason, so why not this, too? Abigail gave Eirwen one head nod.

"I put the sheet music on the piano already," Ian said. "There are two processionals and one recessional. Come with me, Eirwen. I'll show you. There's still a little time to practice before the ceremony."

"We can watch Eilir for you," Isabelle said. "Go ahead and practice."

Eirwen nodded, then followed Ian into the little chapel, and Abigail took Eilir by the hand and led her into the girls' dressing room. The ceremony would start soon. They had less than one hour to get their dresses on and be ready.

Christian greeted Eirwen when she entered the chapel with Ian, then introduced her to his father and Alexander.

"Bad news, Christian. The pianist is sick and can't make it at all. Eirwen has volunteered to play the songs you and Abigail have picked out," Ian said.

"You can play the piano, Eirwen?" Christian asked.

"Well, sort of. My mom taught me how, but as I told everyone else, I have never played in front of an audience."

Christian mulled over the thought of Eirwen trying to play. He wasn't sure it was a very good idea. After a moment he thought, it couldn't hurt to let her practice. Could it be any worse than no music at all? Besides, everything else for this wedding had just fallen into place. Why should this be any different?

"Go ahead and give it a whirl. The sheet music is awaiting you at the piano, along with a wedding program."

Eirwen walked over to the piano, sat down on the bench, and began to study the notes of the songs she would try to play.

"Do you think she can play at all?" Alexander asked.

"Truth be told, I think we're all going to hear a pleasant surprise," Christian said, not taking his eyes from Eirwen.

Eirwen looked over at the four men watching her and gave them a faint, uneasy smile. Noah and Ian took a seat in the first row of the pews, while Christian and Alexander remained standing as they waited. Eirwen put her right foot onto the foot petal, and then she put her long, slender fingers onto the keys. What happened next impressed the four men. Eirwen's delivery was flawless. The sweet sound of the song reverberated through the small chapel. When she was finished playing the first song, complete silence filled the room. None of the men made a sound.

"I'm sorry. Was I bad?" Eirwen asked, sounding anxious.

"That was some of the most extraordinary music I've ever heard come out of this piano," Ian said, ashamed of his earlier doubts.

"Where did you learn to play like that?" Christian asked. "It sounded perfect, the way it rolled out of the piano."

"Like I said, my mom taught me," she explained.

Christian laughed. "Well, you did a fabulous job, that's for certain." He looked down at his watch. "Keep practicing if you wish. We'll finish up our work."

Christian nudged Alexander and pointed to the candles. Alexander nodded, and they started to light them all. When they finished, they grabbed Noah and headed for the men's dressing room. They'd have to rush to get their suits on, as one o'clock was fast approaching.

Ian waited at the entrance to the chapel, greeting the close friends and family who could attend the wedding on such short notice. At five minutes to one, about forty people were seated in the little chapel. Ian went to the women's dressing room and then the men's, letting everyone know with a quiet knock on the door that only a few minutes remained until the ceremony would start.

Christian emerged first, well-dressed in a black suit, white shirt, and white tie. A small, delicate, white rose boutonniere on his jacket lapel represented his mother and her silent presence on this special day. He followed Ian up to the altar, took his place, and waited.

Alexander and Noah waited outside the chapel doors as Abigail, Isabelle, and Eilir emerged from the dressing room with only a minute to spare. Alexander propped open the chapel doors and signaled to his father. Everyone was ready for the ceremony to commence.

Ian looked over to Eirwen seated at the piano and gave her a quick nod. With that, Eirwen started to play the "Prince of Denmark's march." Little Eilir entered the room first. She carried a small wicker basket that contained the white rose petals. Resting in the middle of the basket, a tiny pillow held Abigail and Christian's wedding rings. Eilir tossed white rose petals in the aisle as she walked toward the altar.

Once Eilir reached the front row, Alexander started to escort his mother up the aisle. Isabelle, the matron of honor, wore a light pink dress and carried a bouquet of white and pink roses. Alexander wore a black suit with a white shirt and black tie. His boutonniere was also a white rose. When they reached the altar, Alexander took his place next to Christian, and Isabelle took her place waiting for Abigail.

As Abigail and Noah waited for Eirwen to finish the first processional, Abigail turned to Noah and straightened his white rose boutonniere. She was happy she and Christian had moved the wedding up so Noah could be here with them. A look of contentment filled Noah's eyes. He felt grateful Christian would have Abigail in his life, because soon, he wouldn't be around any longer for his son.

Noah smiled. "I'm so thankful you let me participate in your special day, Abigail. I can't find words to express my gratitude for you moving the wedding date up just for me."

Abigail's eyes moistened. "I did it for you, and I did it for Christian. If you had missed this day, I never would have forgiven myself. Christian needs you here, and so do I," she said, trying not to cry. "Now take me down the aisle, Dad."

When Eirwen finished the first processional, she paused for a moment. Then she started the second, and "The Bridal Chorus" echoed through the chapel. Everyone stood to see Abigail in all of her glory. Noah's step was deliberate, slow, and steady as he escorted Abigail down the aisle to the altar. Once Abigail was in her place next to Christian, Noah moved into position by the front pew. Everyone waited for Eirwen to finish playing the second processional, and when the song ended, the guests took their seats.

Abigail and Christian faced Ian. He would preside over the ceremony, just as he did for Noah and Elizabeth many years before. Abigail could tell Christian was nervous, but her presence quickly calmed him as she reached over and held his hand.

The glorious illumination of one hundred candles cast a romantic mood throughout the chapel, and the faint light that seeped in from the stained-glass window and the skylight above accented the shadows with an indescribable, marvelous splendor. The rain showers had, for now, abated.

Ian started the wedding with the familiar words "Dearly beloved, we are gathered here today..." and all eyes became transfixed on Christian and Abigail. Perhaps this is why not one person noticed the Monarch butterfly resting outside, atop the skylight.

The time had come for Christian and Abigail to say their vows, then put their rings onto each other's fingers. The best man and matron of honor retrieved the rings from Eilir's flower basket, as Christian and Abigail faced each other and prepared to say their tender words of commitment to one another. Abigail went first. She slid Christian's platinum band onto his ring finger as she said her vows to him. Christian went next. He slid Abigail's beautiful band onto her ring finger and said his vows to her.

Elizabeth's elegant old ring and Abigail's breathtaking new ring had been exquisitely amalgamated together by Bear. Soon, Christian and Abigail would be forever united as husband and wife, merged with love, much like Abigail's wedding ring.

"I now pronounce you husband and wife. You may kiss the bride," Ian said.

The two young lovers kissed a magical kiss, and then they faced their family and friends.

"I am pleased to introduce to you Mr. and Mrs. Christian Bryson," Ian said, presenting the newlyweds to the guests seated in the chapel.

Eirwen played the recessional, "The Wedding March," as Christian and Abigail went down the aisle arm in arm, through the chapel doors, and into the main part of the church. Alexander and Isabelle, then Noah and Eilir followed them out.

Ian remained at the altar, waiting for family and friends to exit the chapel. As he did so, the sun broke through the thick cloud cover for a glimmering moment, casting a small, radiant beam through the skylight and onto the altar. Ian looked up just in time to see the beautiful Monarch butterfly take flight and flutter away. Mesmerized, Ian kept looking to the skylight, even though the butterfly was gone. A soft, low rumbling of thunder shook the church ever so slightly, and then the heavens opened up and the heavy rain started to fall again. Ian watched the large raindrops strike the skylight until the last guest filed out. When he left the altar he whistled to himself as he walked down the aisle and went through the chapel doors.

Christian and Abigail waited by the doors. As their friends and family came through, they hugged and thanked each one for attending their special day.

When all the guests had passed by, Alexander walked over to Christian and Abigail. "What are you two going to do now?"

"We're going to a bed and breakfast down in the Twin Cities for a short honeymoon. It's an old tugboat moored on the Mississippi river, transformed into a bed and breakfast several years ago," Abigail said.

"That sounds romantic, but... it can wait," Alexander said with a sly grin.

"Wait for what?" A tinge of uncertainty clung to Abigail's voice.

"For the wedding present I have in store for you two. I'm not a miracle worker, but I coordinated with some members of our congregation to throw you a wedding party. We'll all be eating shortly. A bunch of the church ladies made your wedding cake and prepared what I call a true Minnesota wedding buffet."

"Are we having a potluck dinner for our wedding reception? That is awesome, Alexander!" Abigail hugged her brother. "We didn't even think about doing anything after our ceremony except heading out to the bed and breakfast."

"Wait, Abigail. There's more. Christian and I talked an army buddy of ours into deejaying for your reception. He can only stay until about seven because he has another commitment, but it's better than nothing."

"Wait a minute. You knew all about this, Christian? And you kept it from me?"

"Umm, surprise!" Christian said, forcing an uneasy laugh. "I hope you aren't mad."

Abigail was stunned. She thought after the wedding Christian would take her out to celebrate alone together. This was a surprise. And a delightful one! Abigail hugged both her husband and brother. "You two are wonderful."

Alexander led Abigail and Christian into the banquet hall of the church. The room was small but could accommodate all who attended the ceremony with ease. Tables and chairs tastefully decorated with balloons, streamers, flowers, and candles of every size and color were ready to seat everyone. The pleasant aroma of various casseroles filled every corner of the hall. Abigail was quick to spot the magnificent three-tiered wedding cake in the center of the room and walked over to admire it. This was more than she dreamed a wedding cake could ever be.

A quick tapping on a microphone interrupted Abigail's appreciation of the wedding cake. "Can everyone please take a chair? We'll be serving the food soon, and I would like to say a prayer before we eat," Ian said. Family and friends found their tables and sat down. Ian waited, and when everyone was seated, he led them all in the saying of grace.

After everyone finished eating the fabulous homemade hot dishes, the woman who baked the wedding cake waved Abigail and Christian over to cut the cake. They cut it and served it to their guests, one by one, thanking each person again with sincerity for sharing their special day with them.

Soon, the cake was gone, and everyone pitched in to clear the plates away and move tables to make way for a small dance floor. The celebration was about to get more sentimental: Christian and Abigail shared their first dance to "A Moment Like This," the same song Abigail had sung earlier in the week, just before Christian proposed.

After their first dance, Abigail called her dad up for a father-daughter dance. Ian cried as he danced with his baby girl. He knew she would be happy with Christian for the rest of her days. When Abigail and her dad finished their dance, Alexander made an inspiring toast to the newlyweds, then the dance floor opened to all.

By seven, most family and friends had left. Abigail and Christian said goodbye to Noah, Ian, Elizabeth, Alexander, Eirwen, and Eilir and thanked each one of them for all they had done to make this memorable day even more special. Then, hand in hand, Abigail and Christian left the church, driving away as husband and wife.

Isabelle walked Eirwen and Eilir to their car. She thanked Eirwen for stepping up and playing the piano, then curtsied to Eilir and thanked her for being a beautiful ring bearer and flower girl. Isabelle retrieved a business card from her purse and handed it to Eirwen. "Here's the address. Can you start working for me on Monday?"

"Yes! Thank you so much!" Tears of happiness fell from Eirwen's eyes.

Isabelle grinned. "No, Eirwen. Thank you."

* * *

"What are you doing the rest of the night?" Ian asked Noah. He had caught sight of Noah trying to sneak out the side door.

"If you must know, I'm going to spend the rest of the evening with my wife. I need some alone time with her."

Ian gave his old friend a gentle hug and patted him on the back. "Well, don't stay out too late. Remember, we're expecting you for breakfast in the morning."

Noah nodded to Ian, then resumed his course out the side door to his car. On the drive to the cemetery, he stopped at home and went into his office. He dialed the combination on the safe, opened it, and removed a yellowish envelope. Holding the brittle envelope with care, Noah looked down at it and reflected on how he had found it on the kitchen table when he returned home after

Christian's birth. Elizabeth had secretly put it there before they left for the hospital.

Inside the envelope was a key to her purpose and a letter he didn't need to read again since he knew the words by heart. The tears that had fallen from his grief-stricken eyes long ago stained the letter, smearing the once unambiguous, tender words into a barely legible blur. The items in the faded envelope, locked up tight in Noah's safe and kept hidden from Christian, would not remain a secret for much longer. Noah put the envelope in his suit pocket and left his house. He hopped into his car and drove to the cemetery to see his wife.

"Purpose" lingered in Noah's thoughts as he drove out of sight.

Chapter 11

BED AND BREAKFAST

"There she is," Christian said to Abigail, nodding in the general direction of the floating tugboat.

"Wow, it's cool. I can't wait to see the inside of it." Abigail paused a moment, taking in the serene beauty of the tugboat and the surrounding Mississippi River.

The tugboat, painted for the most part in white, had black railings guarding the decking and was a majestic three stories tall. The Mighty Mississippi River rolled by in the background, its murky waves caressing the tugboat floating gracefully upon its waters. The tugboat seemed to snuggle into the river, as if they coexisted in quiet harmony.

When the newlyweds arrived, Christian carried the luggage down the long wooden pier. Their stay would last only a few days, but Abigail's suitcase was much heavier than his. Why a woman packed two weeks worth of clothes for a short two-day vacation was mind-boggling to Christian, but he decided it would not be wise to pick a fight on his wedding day. It would be a losing battle, anyway. Now nearing eight in the evening, the outer lights came on to illuminate the skeleton of the ship. The ship all lit up, with the river and the bright city lights in the background, was a breathtaking sight for the newlyweds to witness.

Christian and Abigail entered the inn through two sets of double doors and lost themselves in the romantic ambiance of the tugboat's cozy salon. The salon was a small room, but it served a dual purpose: guests could check in there for their evenings of romance, and it doubled as an eating area where breakfast was served to guests who stayed overnight.

The salon featured four small tables and chairs spaced throughout the room, offering coziness and privacy. Both sides of the salon sported several windows, which helped illuminate the room. For a room on a boat, it was light, airy, and elegant. A gas fireplace roared on the outer bulkhead of the salon, adding to its romantic flavor even more. By the check-in desk, a spiral staircase stretched up and down through the deck floors, leading to the four private rooms.

Christian and Abigail rang the bell at the check-in desk. An older woman emerged through another set of doors that led to the tugboat's galley. She was slender with silver hair and a fair complexion, and appeared nicely settled into what was now the autumn of her life. She looked at the newlyweds with endearment in her eyes. Christian was still wearing his suit and Abigail her elegant white wedding dress.

"Hello! My name is Pearl and I'm the sole proprietor of this floating establishment. Welcome to my humble home."

"Thank you very much," Abigail and Christian said at the same time.

Pearl smiled. "You're welcome. And also, congratulations are in order to you both on your special day."

Once Pearl checked in Christian and Abigail for their stay, she escorted them up the spiral staircase to the stateroom they'd be staying in for the next couple of nights. Pearl unlocked the set of double doors to their stateroom and then handed Christian the key.

"If you need anything at all, I'll be down in the salon for a few more hours. Breakfast will be served from seven until ten in the morning." Pearl shut the doors behind her, leaving the two lovebirds alone.

Abigail and Christian were awestruck by the exquisite beauty of the stateroom. The warm and welcoming room was luxurious and romantic beyond their wildest dreams. The room's woodwork and paneling were gorgeous. The oak hardwood floors, stained a beautiful, deep golden brown, made the room feel cozy. Above, oak beams supported the ceiling with stylish grace. The gas fireplace on the wall emitted a soft, romantic glow that added to the handsome ambience of the stateroom. Two red, oversized chairs and a coffee table rested atop a hand-woven Persian rug and faced the soft glowing flames that flickered from the fireplace. On top of the coffee table was a clear crystal vase containing a dozen white roses, along with a box of fine Belgian chocolates and a bottle of sparkling champagne chilling in an ice bucket.

Delighted, Abigail and Christian smiled at each other. Above all else, they were elated at being alone in silence after their long, hectic day. The room had no telephone or television. Abigail and Christian had left their cell phones at home on purpose so they wouldn't be disturbed on their honeymoon.

Abigail gave Christian a warm hug and soft kiss, happy to have him all to herself, alone together, at last. "I'm going to take a quick shower and freshen up. Can you please pour me a glass of champagne?"

"But you're still underage," Christian teased, shaking his head.

"Only for a few more months, my love. Then I'll be the same age as you." Abigail slugged her new husband in the arm. She picked up her suitcase and took it with her into the bathroom, shutting and locking the door behind her.

Christian proceeded to close all the wood blinds to the room's windows and outer deck doors. He dimmed the lights to cast an even more romantic mood. Then he walked over to the coffee table and uncorked the champagne. He poured some into two glasses and then took a seat in one of the chairs in front of the fireplace. Christian drank down his first glass of champagne in one swift gulp, then poured another glass and waited for Abigail to emerge from the bathroom. His eyes fixed for a bit on the hypnotizing flames dancing from the fireplace log. That's why he didn't hear Abigail tiptoe up behind him. She covered his eyes with her hands and blew her warm breath into his right ear.

"Guess who?" Abigail purred in a low whisper that tickled his ear.

"I'm guessing my beautiful bride who I know is dying to make love to her husband for the very first time," Christian replied.

"Ding, ding, ding, we have a winner. Let's see what our lucky contestant has won… oh, your prize is me," Abigail bantered. She uncovered Christian's eyes and walked around to sit on his lap.

Abigail wore a red lacy teddy that hugged her delicate and petite body. She had bought the teddy extra-small on purpose so her chest would bust out. Her game plan was to drive Christian insane with desire. However, she could have donned a burlap sack and Christian still would've wanted her just the same. Abigail gave him a long passionate kiss, then took her glass of champagne from the coffee table and downed it in one gulp. The champagne's delicate bubbles tickled Abigail's nose like soft feathers.

Abigail bit her lower lip. "Make love to me now, my handsome husband," she said, her voice low, and sexy.

Christian stood up from the chair and carried Abigail over to the queen-size bed. He laid her down on the soft, white satin sheets. Then Christian undressed. He was slow and deliberate as he removed his clothes, and Abigail watched with quiet excitement. On the outside, she was calm, but on the inside, she was ready to explode, like an active volcano's impending eruption.

Christian moved above her and kissed her all over. His lips were warm and tender. He softly pressed them against Abigail's body: her lips, her nose, her ears, her neck, her arms, her stomach, her legs, and her feet. Abigail wanted him more and more with each sensual kiss. Christian administered a dose of medicine with each one of his kisses, like a temporary remedy he and only he could provide to treat Abigail's deep desire for his love. There was, however, no cure for his love, nor did she want one.

Christian removed Abigail's little red teddy. He paused a moment to appreciate her beauty as the romantic glow of the fireplace cast their silhouettes upon the wall. Then the two young souls, who had loved each other for as long as they could remember, made love to one another, and their hearts fused into one.

Night had settled in, veiling the sky in complete darkness. Christian and Abigail were both exhausted. Their energy was spent from the long day, and the sensual lovemaking was the icing on the cake. Abigail rolled to her side and Christian snuggled up behind her. He put his arms around her and held her tight, letting her know he would be there forever. Nestled alone, together at last, they both faded fast asleep to the gentle pitter-patter of the cool evening rain that had started falling ever-so-lightly from the heaven above.

After some time, Abigail awoke from her deep slumber to find Christian missing from the bed. She wrapped the sheets around herself in a hurry and got up. She turned the bedside lamp on, which blinded her as her eyes tried to adjust to the brightness of the room. She struggled to focus, her head still groggy from just awakening. Abigail squinted at the clock: two in the morning and Christian was nowhere in the room. Then she spotted the door to their promenade deck slightly ajar. She walked to it and pulled the door open to find Christian standing naked against the deck railing. His hair and body, soaked by the cold early morning drizzle, glistened in the shadows of the tugboat's exterior lights.

"Christian, what are you doing?" Abigail asked, disbelieving what she was seeing.

Christian didn't reply. He stared out to the river with a blank, expressionless gaze. Even though he was standing just in front of Abigail, mentally he was in some other place. Abigail, troubled by his lack of response, stepped into the rain and pulled him back into the stateroom by the arm. He was freezing, his lips trembling and slightly blue. Seeing Christian like this worried Abigail and she acted, without hesitation. She dragged Christian into the bathroom, turned on the shower, forced Christian in, and stepped in with him. Abigail rubbed her hands on Christian's body, frantic to warm him fast. Christian's face was still expressionless, as if he were in a deep zombie-like trance. The hot water beat down on both of them, and Abigail started to cry. What was wrong with him? Her tears fell, like the hot water, and swirled down the drain and out of sight.

Christian snapped out of his comatose state. He realized Abigail was sobbing, and he pulled her to his chest and held her tight while the hot water cascaded down on them both. "I'm so sorry, Abigail. I just lost it, there." He begged for her forgiveness, continuing to hold her in his arms as she quaked with a fear unlike anything he'd ever experienced.

"Never scare me like that again, Christian, ever!" Abigail's squeaky voice cracked. After a long moment, she looked into his eyes. "Would you like to talk about what just happened?"

"Yes, we can. Let's get out of the shower and towel off first."

They dried off and Abigail rushed to the inviting warmth of the queen-sized bed. Christian retrieved something from his suitcase, sat down at the foot of the bed, and rolled the covers back to expose Abigail's feet.

Abigail laughed. "Do I dare ask why you had that in your suitcase?" A big smile covered her face as she pointed to the bottle of pink nail polish in Christian's hand.

"I'm going to paint your little toes." he said, smiling.

"Well, I would have married you a lot sooner if I'd known you painted toenails." She wiggled her toes with glee, then adjusted the pillows behind her back to get more comfortable and put her feet on Christians lap.

Christian shook the bottle of polish for a few seconds, then opened it and started to paint Abigail's right big toenail.

"Why were you standing outside in the cold drizzle? Did something scare you?" Abigail asked softly.

Christian didn't look up. He kept his eyes focused on her feet while he painted her toenails pink. "Yes, I was frightened. I thought about the inevitability of losing my dad and being all alone. But in the hot shower, my mind thawed and I realized as long as we have each other, I'll never be alone."

"Christian, look me in the eyes," Abigail pleaded.

He paused, and then looked up into her soft, light blue eyes.

"I promise I will always be here for you as long as you let me be. You can count on it."

Christian smiled as he looked into her eyes. He knew Abigail's promises were as good as gold, which comforted his uneasiness.

"It appears I don't have a promising future as a toenail-painting technician." Christian looked back down to his horrendous work, and chuckled.

"They look perfect to me. Now let's get a little rest. I'd like to do some shopping later today if that's okay with you, mister." She wiggled her toes again and smiled, delighted by her husband's handiwork.

Christian turned off the bedside lights and settled in under the blanket next to Abigail. He cupped himself around her as they both drifted off to sleep.

Abigail and Christian slept in until shortly after nine. They woke and dressed, smiling at one another. Abigail opened all the stateroom's window blinds, letting in the new morning's splendid sunlight.

"It's clearing up outside, Christian. It should be a glorious day to go shopping," Abigail announced. Her spirits were high and nothing was going to put a damper on her day. "Come on, sleepy head. Get your butt moving so we can eat some breakfast in the salon."

Christian and Abigail sat down at a table by the window close to the fireplace. Outside they could see other boats and barges steering their way along The Mighty Mississippi River. The delectable aroma of eggs, bacon, and pancakes oozed through the tugboat's galley doors and wafted in the air all around them, awakening their yearning taste buds. Both Christian and Abigail were famished and would've eaten just about anything served to them this morning. They hadn't eaten anything in sixteen hours, except for the Belgian chocolates and the sparkling champagne.

They were alone in the salon. Pearl greeted them with an endearing smile, then served them breakfast, catering to their every wish, as if they were royalty. The pampering they received was bar none.

"My dear, where do you put all your food?" Pearl asked Abigail. She was amazed this petite young woman could pack away the food with such ferocity.

"I think my beautiful bride has a tapeworm," Christian jibed.

"I do believe you're right," Pearl concurred with a hearty laugh, smiling at the couple. The phone at the check-in desk started to ring. "Excuse me while I answer that."

"What would you like to do after shopping this morning, Abigail?"

"Maybe we can spend the late afternoon at the Museum of Art or something along those lines. I also heard the Science Museum has an excellent music exhibit from the early days of mankind."

Pearl came back to their table. "Excuse me, Mrs. Bryson. I'm sorry to interrupt, but you have a phone call. He says it's urgent."

Abigail rushed to the phone. Christian's eyes never wavered from her.

"This is Abigail," she said.

"Abigail, it's your dad," Ian said, his voice somber.

"What's wrong, Dad?" Abigail asked, worried. Her eyes locked onto Christian.

"You need to tell Christian, dear. His father lost his battle with cancer sometime late last night."

Abigail's eyes welled up with tears. Christian, his eyes still upon hers, knew what the call was about. He came to the harsh realization he was now parentless. Abigail ended the conversation with her father and rushed to Christian. She sat on his lap and hugged him tight while they both cried.

Abigail had known this moment would one day come, but now that it was upon her she felt helpless. Christian's heart needed her consoling, but she knew it didn't matter what she said. Any words spoken to Christian were immaterial at the moment. All she could do was hold him and love him with all her heart. Time would ease his heartache and sorrow, and Abigail dedicated herself as the buffer between now and then.

Chapter 12

TOMORROW NEVER COMES

Christian and Abigail packed their suitcases in silence. Their honeymoon was over. They could've stayed another night, but their special time couldn't continue after the devastating news of Noah's death.

Abigail did her best to console Christian in his time of bereavement, but he was distant, lost in his unfathomable thoughts. Together they left the bed and breakfast with a wealth of great memories, and a couple of terrible ones. Their honeymoon, though brief, would be forever imprinted into their minds.

The long walk from the bed and breakfast down the pier to Christian's truck was painful for them both. Their hearts were heavy as they walked into the stiff wind that had just started to blow. When they reached the truck, Abigail offered to drive home, but Christian declined. He needed something to do to keep his mind occupied.

The conversation on the short journey home was at a minimum. Abigail massaged the back of Christian's neck the entire drive, trying diligently to ease his soul as she struggled with her own heartache.

Christian parked his truck on the gravel driveway of Ian and Isabelle's house. They both sat in silence for a moment, and then Christian turned to Abigail and gave her a soft, tender kiss. He slid out, walked around the front of his truck, and opened her door. Abigail knew Christian's subtle actions were his way of thanking her for the love she had shown him today, especially for the tender neck massage on the ride home. Abigail also knew if Christian did try to speak any words of gratitude, he would break down in tears.

They slowly walked up the cobblestone sidewalk, up the porch stairs, and into the house. Ian and Isabelle met the two of them with open arms. All four of them huddled together and hugged each other for several minutes, crying together. The Havilys were now the only family Christian had left. The solace they provided him in his time of need was comforting to his soul. Christian knew losing his dad would be hard, but he never expected it to drown his heart in complete sorrow.

After a long, poignant, emotional group hug, Christian pulled himself away from the comforting embrace of Ian, Isabelle, and Abigail. He dried his eyes with his shirtsleeve and composed himself as best he could while pulling up a chair at the dining room table. He rested his weary head on the table. The grief he was enduring was an exhausting, debilitating emotional drain.

"I am sorry, son," Ian said with graceful compassion. He rested his hand on the back of Christian's head.

"I'm sorry, too," Isabelle said. She rubbed Christian's back. "If there is anything we can do to help ease your suffering, please let us know."

Christian thought for a moment, searching for what could eradicate the horrid feeling in his heart. Devastated, he knew he couldn't go back to his dad's house.

"Abigail and I were planning on house hunting after our honeymoon, but my heart won't be in it for a while. Is there any chance we could stay here for a few days? I'd appreciate not having to stay at my dad's place."

"You can stay here as long as you need, Christian. You're family," Isabelle replied, continuing to rub his back with a motherly love.

"Thank you both very much," Christian said, relieved he didn't have to venture into his dad's house today. It would've been just too much to endure.

Ian motioned for Abigail and Isabelle to take a seat at the table. Christian picked his head up off the table and did his best to make eye contact with Abigail and his in-laws. Abigail reached over and held his hand, comforting Christian with her soothing touch.

"Where did he die?" Christian asked. He was hoping the response would help make him feel at ease inside.

"Your dad didn't show up for breakfast this morning, so I went to check on him at home. When I didn't find him there, I remembered he had mentioned as he was leaving the wedding reception he was going to visit your mom at the cemetery. I found him this morning, lying next to your mother's grave. He looked at peace," Ian said.

"I can't think of any other way my dad would've wanted to go. His love for my mom was unwavering until his last dying breath."

"I believe your mom and dad wanted you to have this." Ian removed a faded yellow envelope from his jacket pocket and slid it across the table to Christian.

"What is this?" Christian inquired.

"That, I do not know. I didn't open it. It belongs to you, Christian. Your dad had it clutched in his hands when I found him."

Christian looked down at the envelope and the faded handwriting on the front. It had only two names on it: Noah and Christian. Christian picked it up with trembling hands. He stared at it for a moment, then looked to Abigail and his in-laws. He opened the envelope, not knowing what to expect.

Inside was a single sheet of paper folded into thirds, with something hard tucked inside. When he opened the correspondence his mother had left for his dad and himself, a skeleton key dropped to the table. The key, made of what looked like pewter, was intricate in contour and design. The shaft ran narrow and long, with five levers on the end. The head appeared handcrafted, meticulous in construction, painstakingly forged in the shape of a butterfly. Orange, black, and white gems decorated the wings, casting a subtle illusion of a Monarch butterfly.

Christian held the key up so everyone at the table could get a better look at it. Ian, Isabelle, and Abigail ogled in awe and wonderment. The key's splendorous beauty was breathtaking.

"What do you suppose the key is for, Christian?" Abigail asked. Her eyes were still transfixed on the beautiful butterfly key.

"I suppose I should read the letter out loud and we can all find out," Christian said, clearing his throat. He concentrated on the faded words the letter contained. Droplets, perhaps left by his dad's sorrowful tears, lightly stained the paper. Christian began to read his mother's calligraphy aloud, a faint smile spreading over his face as he spoke...

To my dearest Noah and Christian,

My precious loves, this letter is for both of you. Noah, I know it will be difficult for you to accept I am now gone. I hope you will be able to find it in your heart to come visit me as I rest eternally in my grave. I need you to do a special deed for me, though, an important purpose I now bestow upon you. Please make sure Christian receives this letter and butterfly key, for he is the only one who can use the key when the time is right.

Christian hesitated, taking time to reflect on the butterfly key before he continued reading his mother's words …

Christian, this butterfly key holds the answers to all the questions that are still unanswered, and the answers to all the questions that have yet to be asked. In time, you will find the solution to all your questions, ultimately leading you to your extraordinary purpose. Until that day comes, however, you will not know what purpose the butterfly key serves. Do not lose your faith in me, though. Eventually you will know, understand, and believe in what seemed impossible to comprehend at first.

I love you both always and forever,
Elizabeth

Christian folded up the letter and put the butterfly key inside. He then placed it inside the faded yellow envelope with the utmost care. He looked to his wife and in-laws sitting stupefied in their chairs. Each one of their faces projected a silent apprehension that betrayed their thoughts.

"Well, now I have more questions than answers," Christian joked. "Maybe the key does open something, or maybe, just maybe, it's nothing more than a symbolic icon representing my mother's love and literally doesn't unlock anything. I'll be delighted just the same whether the key does or doesn't open anything at all. I'm just so happy to have an heirloom to cherish that once belonged to my mother. Now, if it's okay with all of you, I would like to take a nap. I'm drained." He stood up from the table and excused himself.

"So would I," Abigail said. She yawned and stretched as she excused herself from the table.

"Okay kids, get some rest. Abigail, take your husband up to your bedroom. The room now belongs to both of you," Isabelle stated.

Abigail and Christian trudged up the flight of stairs, slow in their journey to their bedroom. Both their bodies and minds were drained from events of the past twenty-four hours, and they collapsed onto Abigail's bed without regard to the fact they were still dressed. Christian rolled onto his side and Abigail snuggled up behind. It was her turn to hold him now, and hold him she did as he cried himself to sleep.

* * *

In the three days leading up to Noah's funeral, Christian tried to keep busy, but it was difficult for him to focus. His mind teetered on the edge of a breakdown whenever he saw any of his dad's belongings. Only two things made the days bearable for Christian: Abigail's never-ending love and her infinite patience. Without her, he would've been lost in sorrow.

Noah had prearranged all of his funeral wishes with Ian and Isabelle so Christian wouldn't feel overwhelmed or burdened by all the responsibilities. All Noah wanted was a simple graveside burial and memorial, no wake or formal funeral in the church at all. He wanted to rest with Elizabeth as soon as possible. Ian and Isabelle carried out his dying wishes with the utmost diligence.

As family and close friends attended the graveside burial, the skies were a deep crystal blue. Puffy, white clouds, like pillows, floated above head. The weather was ideal in every sense. Christian found the weather somewhat ironic: It had rained on a day of complete joy, his wedding, and it was picture perfect on a day of utter sorrow, his dad's funeral.

Ian presided over the burial ceremony for his close, dear friend. His eulogy seemed miraculous, as divine inspiration resonated deep in each word he spoke. Ian's speech and delivery could move mountains and divide the seas. However, hidden deep down inside Ian's spirit, a perilous battle was just beginning.

For the first time in his life, doubt had crept into Ian's soul, and the innocent belief of a greater purpose in life started to bleed out of his heart. The doubt acted like a slow leak in a neglected hot air balloon, unnoticeable at first, but disastrous if left unattended, resulting in a demoralizing collapse. Ian's faith and convictions were starting to falter little by little with each passing beat of his heart. His strong will struggled to fight the numbness, but the hopeless feeling welling deep inside him was more than he could handle alone. Ian's spirit spiraled, heading toward perilous danger, and without the divine intervention he would soon pray for, his heart would rend asunder.

When the eulogy was over, Ian led family and friends in the Lord's Prayer as Noah's body was lowered to his final resting place next to his beloved wife. Christian was the first person to sprinkle a handful of earth onto his dad's casket. Then, one by one, everyone at the service repeated Christian's actions.

When the service concluded, family and friends left and went to Ian and Isabelle's home for a celebration of Noah's life. Christian and Abigail stayed behind. Christian needed a little more time for closure with his parents, and Abigail just wanted to support her husband in his time of need.

Christian sat down on the old faded bench by the foot of his parents' graves, and Abigail joined him, sympathetically putting her arms around him.

"Would you like to tell me what is on your mind, my love?" she asked.

"It's weird. Everything seems so final. I mean, what is the purpose of life? Is it to live and to die? What happens next?" A look of hopelessness and defeat enveloped his face.

"The purpose is not to just live and die. The purpose is all those days in between and what you choose to do with them, to live as a fine human being, and to touch other lives in a positive way, like you did for Eilir on your birthday. That was your day and you sacrificed yourself to make it her special day. Your actions affected Eilir's heart. She'll carry those memories with her the rest of her life. And that, Christian, is your purpose, to make a profound impact on all the lives you touch."

Christian pondered Abigail's words long and hard. She always seemed to know the answers to everything, which eased his soul. He felt grateful Abigail was there with him through everything, especially when he learned of his dad's death. He didn't know how he could ever live without Abigail. The realization of the heartache and sorrow his father had known for twenty-one years without his mother took hold of Christian. Finally, he understood the pain his father had endured.

"I promise you whenever you need me, I'll be there for you, Abigail, just like you have always been here for me," Christian said, hugging his wife.

After a long, silent embrace, Abigail said, "I suppose we should head home to join the celebration of life for your father."

Christian gazed upon his parents' graves for just a few seconds more. He then smiled, knowing they would rest beside each other, together, forever at last.

"Okay, let's head back home." Christian stood up and took Abigail by the hand. "Goodbye, Mom and Dad, I love you both."

Christian and Abigail turned and strolled arm in arm to Christian's truck. Even though it was a sad day, Christian was happy, and so were the two Monarch butterflies frolicking in the milkweed patch nearby.

Chapter 13

DOG DAYS OF AUGUST

The long, scorching dog days of summer in Columbus, Minnesota are comparable to cooking oneself in a sweltering steam bath. Any rain that happened to fall just made conditions more unbearable, like tossing cold water onto the burning hot coals of a sauna. The sultry humidity that followed the thunderstorms would stick to the skin like leeches, sucking life right out of anyone lingering outside.

The rain that had fallen all night had abated around five in the morning. The mercury was rising on outdoor thermometers throughout the town, and so was the brutal humidity. Such were the miserable conditions Christian and Alexander faced for the weekend's Army National Guard training.

"Wow! It's hot as hell out here!" Christian said, looking at his truck's temperature gauge. The reading was a balmy eighty-eight degrees at seven in the morning.

"I don't mind the heat. It's the humidity I can't stand. My uniform sticks to my back and makes my skin crawl." Alexander put his face closer to the air conditioning vents in Christian's truck, trying without success to dry the perspiration on his brow.

Christian laughed. "I'll take the heat anytime over the freezing winter weather." He pulled into the parking lot of the army reserve center and looked in vain for a parking space in the shade.

Christian and Alexander didn't want to open the truck doors. They knew the searing humidity outside would hit them like a hard punch in the gut. The hot air was difficult to breathe as they retrieved their duffle bags from the back of the truck and made their way into the comfort of the air-conditioned barracks. As they were storing their gear, a voice rang out behind them.

"Specialist Bryson, Specialist Havily, come with me. The Colonel is waiting for you in his office," Lieutenant Kabecka ordered.

"Yes, sir!" they replied and fell in step behind the Lieutenant.

* * *

Abigail awoke soon after Christian and Alexander left for their weekend army training. The moment she sat up, the room started to spin and she was nauseous. She raced to the bathroom and made it to the toilet, barely. She vomited several times, but her stomach still ached, as if she had swallowed a huge rock and it remained wedged inside her tummy. The waves of nausea passed after a few minutes, but Abigail still felt a little woozy, and she was sweating profusely. Something was wrong. She had always been a healthy person. She had no fever, no body aches, and no diarrhea, just what seemed like an enormous rock, lodged inside her tummy.

After a few minutes, Abigail stood up and walked into her bedroom, her steps slow and deliberate. She dressed herself in shorts and a tee shirt and then walked downstairs. Next she put on her shoes, and grabbed a water bottle from the refrigerator. Then Abigail retrieved her car keys from the kitchen counter, slung her purse over her shoulder, and went out the front door. The high heat and humidity made her feel nauseated again, and she wished one of her parents were home to take her to her private doctor in town. But since they were both working, she would have to drive herself.

Just as Abigail arrived at the clinic parking lot and stepped out of her car, she vomited again. She stumbled toward the entrance of the clinic and fainted, collapsing just a few feet from the front door. Two young men saw her fall and rushed to her aid. They picked her up and carried her inside, where the doctor's staff instructed them to place her on an emergency room bed.

After a few minutes, Abigail started to come around. She was surprised to find herself in a bed, with fluids from an intravenous drip going into her left arm.

"Hello, Abigail," Dr. Carter said. He meticulously flashed his light into her eyes to check the dilation of her pupils. "Welcome back. You gave us quite a scare, there."

Dr. Carter had been Abigail's personal doctor since she was thirteen. He was tall, dark, and handsome, approximately in his late thirties. His demeanor reflected his fastidious nature, as he showed great care and attention to all of his patients' wellbeing. Abigail was reassured to see him. His presence always calmed her nerves.

"Hello, Dr. Carter. I'm not feeling so well today." Abigail licked her dry lips. "Is there any chance I can get a glass of cold water?"

"Sorry. Not until we find out what's wrong. As you can see, we have an intravenous line delivering some fluids. For the moment, we're treating you for dehydration because you fainted from the high heat. Can you tell me what other symptoms you're experiencing?"

"I don't think I'm dehydrated at all. All my symptoms started as I got out of bed this morning. I sat up and a wave of dizziness and nausea swept over me, and then I vomited for several minutes. To tell the truth, I feel like someone just kicked me in the stomach."

Dr. Carter took out his stethoscope and listened to Abigail's tummy. Then he felt her stomach with his gentle touch.

"Did you have any blood in your vomit?" he asked, pushing lightly into her belly.

"No."

"I don't want to startle you, but there is an off chance you could be pregnant. We drew some blood when you were unconscious, and the results should be ready in about fifteen minutes. In the meantime, I'll have the nurse get you some ice chips to suck on. And I'll put some medication in the IV line to combat your nausea."

"Pregnant!" Abigail stumbled on the word. Disbelief overwhelmed her. She never even thought about becoming pregnant this fast.

"I said it was possible, Abigail. It could very well be the stomach flu. Just try to rest. We should have your test results back soon."

* * *

Christian and Alexander followed Lieutenant Kabecka into Colonel Andrews' office and then stood at attention in front of his desk.

"Sir, Specialist Bryson and Specialist Havily are here as you requested."

"Thank you, Lieutenant. Please shut the door on the way out. You are dismissed."

"Yes, sir." Lieutenant Kabecka did an about face and left the room, shutting the door behind himself.

"At ease, gentlemen, and pull up a seat," Colonel Andrews said, pointing to the two chairs in front of his desk.

Christian and Alexander sat down and waited for the Colonel to tell them why he had summoned them.

Colonel Andrews, a well-respected officer, loved by all the men who served under him, was a compassionate family man above all else. His doors were always open to soldiers who needed to sit down and just talk about any problems they might be experiencing. The Colonel was also an excellent listener, and if he couldn't help fix a problem, he'd for damn sure find someone who could. Colonel Andrews wasn't of the typical military mold. He often bent the rules ever so slightly during special circumstances if it benefited the men he commanded.

"I'd like to say I'm sorry for the loss of your father, Specialist Bryson. Also to you, Specialist Havily. I hear Mr. Bryson was like a second father to you."

"Thank you, sir," both Christian and Alexander said.

"You're welcome, gentleman. Are you both okay to once again serve your country?"

"Yes, sir," Christian and Alexander replied simultaneously.

"Very well then, gentlemen. I have special deployment orders for you both. They came in roughly three weeks ago, but somehow I misplaced them until now." The Colonel gave the boys a sly smile and a wink.

Christian and Alexander nodded to the Colonel to show their gratitude for delaying their deployment orders on purpose during their time of mourning.

"I have to get you boys moving now or the court martial I'd probably face for delaying you both would force me into retirement. Your orders, men, will station you at a top-secret espionage base deep inside Afghanistan. Due to the sensitive location and nature of the information gathered there, telephone and computer access is strictly off limits. The only contact you can have with the outside world will be through the U.S. mail.

"Your primary duty assignment will be the securing of the checkpoint located on the only road leading to and from the base. Our unit must operate the checkpoint and roadblock twenty-four hours a day. Roughly two weeks ago, thirty-four other Red Bulls were deployed, along with two lieutenants. You two, along with Lieutenant Kabecka, will be leaving here tomorrow morning for a one-year tour of duty. You will report to my office no later than zero-nine-hundred hours. Is that understood?"

"Yes, sir," Christian and Alexander simultaneously replied.

"I apologize for the short notice, gentlemen, but you should have been gone a few weeks ago. This was the best I could do." Colonel Andrews stood up and smiled at the two young men before him.

"Thank you, sir," Christian and Alexander said. They stood and extended their hands to him.

"Good luck, gentleman, and Godspeed." The Colonel extended his hand back to them and shook their hands, his grip firm. "You are dismissed."

Christian and Alexander returned to the barracks and retrieved their duffle bags, then made the trip home for what would be the last day with their families for one entire year.

* * *

Dr. Carter knocked on the door and entered Abigail's room. He carried the clipboard containing Abigail's medical charts along with the test results of her blood work.

"Good news, Mrs. Bryson. Your test results came back positive. You're pregnant. Congratulations. You're an expectant mother!"

Abigail was taken aback by this news, and excited. She couldn't believe getting pregnant would be this easy. The conception of this baby must have happened on the night of their honeymoon. She and Christian were not trying to get pregnant. Christian wasn't ready, and Abigail wasn't going to push the issue until he was.

"You can get dressed now. Please stop at the appointment desk on your way out. I'd like to see you in about six weeks to check on the progress of your pregnancy." Dr. Carter removed her intravenous line, then handed her a prescription for a medication to help alleviate her nausea.

"Thank you, Dr. Carter," Abigail said.

She waited for him to leave the room, then jumped off the hospital bed and dressed as fast as she could. She and Christian would soon be parents, just as they had promised each other!

Chapter 14

VEILED FORTUNES

Christian and Alexander returned home around ten o'clock to an empty house. Ian and Isabelle were still at work, and Abigail was nowhere around.

"Would you like a soda, Christian?" Alexander asked as he rummaged through the refrigerator.

"Naw, but I'll take a bottle of water if you've got one."

"One ice cold bottle of water coming right up. Here, catch." Alexander tossed the chilly bottle to Christian.

With beverages in hand, Christian and Alexander made their way to the dining room. Alexander grabbed the kitchen telephone off the hook and brought it with him.

"I suppose we'd better call my parents and break the news to them. How do you think Abigail will take it?" Alexander asked.

"I don't know, but I'd put a ton of money on her not being very happy about it," Christian replied, a worried look crossing his face.

As Abigail drove up the driveway to the house, she saw Christian's truck and wondered why he was home already. He wasn't supposed to return home until Monday. At least now she could tell him about her pregnancy, much earlier than she'd anticipated. Abigail parked her car, raced up the sidewalk, and flew through the front door.

"Christian, where are you?" Abigail shouted, unable to contain her excitement.

"We're in the dining room!" he yelled back.

Abigail rushed into the dining room and found Christian and her twin brother sitting at table, heads hanging low.

"Christian, I have some good news and… um, what's wrong? You two look pretty downhearted."

"You'd better break the news to her. I'm going to call Mom and Dad to let them know what's happening," Alexander said to Christian. He got up and walked into the kitchen with the telephone.

Christian watched Alexander until he was out of sight, then focused his attention on Abigail.

"Break what to me?" Abigail put both of her hands on her stomach and rubbed her tummy in small, gentle circles to help ease the qualm she was now feeling deep inside.

"We received deployment orders today. We're being activated to Afghanistan for a year."

Abigail's heart sank. She sat down at the table, trying to comprehend what Christian had just told her.

"A year?" Abigail asked, hoping she hadn't heard him correctly.

"Yes, I'm afraid so. A year. The news gets worse, my love. Our mission is top secret. We received explicit orders; we can't have any direct contact with family or friends during our deployment over there. Any computer access or telephone conversation by us is an infraction of the rules, strictly prohibited, and could result in punishment or even court martial. The only communication I can have with you will come through letters in the U.S. mail." Christian looked into her eyes, his sadness unmistakable. "So… you have some good news for me, my love?"

Abigail became sick to her stomach as she struggled to find the words to tell him she was pregnant. All of a sudden, her mind flashed back to Christian standing naked in the cold drizzle the night on the tugboat. She remembered in vivid detail how Christian lost it and how he couldn't function, and she decided to do something she had never done before. She lied to protect Christian from himself.

"I was going to tell you I found a house for sale we'd both love," Abigail said. She avoided making eye contact, afraid that Christian would see right through her deception.

"I guess we're just going to have to wait to look at houses until I return." Christian stood up from the table. "I'm running over to Dad's house to get a few extra things I need. I'll be back soon."

Abigail didn't say anything more as Christian left. She was relieved he hadn't caught her in a lie because she knew it was better this way. However, someone did catch her untruthfulness, and he wasted no time calling her on it.

"I have two things to tell you, Abigail," Alexander said. He stood behind her in the entryway of the dining room. "One: Mom and Dad will be home in less than an hour. Two: I could see right through you when you were lying to Christian. What are you hiding from him?"

Abigail hadn't realized her brother was nearby, but somehow she felt relieved he was there. She needed him, and right now, she wanted to confide in him.

Alexander sat down next to her. "What's going on?" Alexander looked right into her light blue eyes. He could tell with ease his sister was upset, and for a reason other than hearing the news of his and Christian's deployment to Afghanistan.

Abigail pleaded. "Alexander, swear to me with your life you won't tell Christian what I'm about to tell you. You must promise me you won't say a word to him, no matter what."

"It's that bad, huh? Okay, but there'd better be a damn good reason for you not wanting him to know. I don't like keeping secrets."

"Alexander, I'm pregnant," she blurted out.

"Wow. That's great news! Why wouldn't you want to tell Christian he's going to be a daddy?" A puzzled look covered Alexander's face.

Abigail went on to tell her brother what had happened the night of their honeymoon on the tugboat, how she had found Christian standing outside naked in the cold drizzle and had to warm him in the hot shower. Finally, she told her brother about how Christian had been worrying about his father and that was what had caused his mind to lose itself.

"Alexander, Christian needs to have his mind focused on his job. He doesn't need to worry about anything here at home. If he knows I'm pregnant, he could unconsciously endanger himself. I just want him to come home safe to me." Abigail started to cry.

"So be it. Against my better judgment, I won't tell Christian, because that's what your heart desires, even though I disagree with it. I'll promise you something that might help to ease your soul. I'll watch out for Christian every day and protect him. I'll make sure he comes home alive and safe to you and your baby. This, Abigail, I promise you," Alexander vowed.

"Thank you." She reached over and hugged her brother, crying while she did so.

"It's okay, Abigail, everything will be okay." He rubbed her back and comforted her the best he knew how.

Soon Christian returned from his dad's house. He found Abigail crying into Alexander's arms at the dining room table. When Abigail noticed Christian standing beside her, she went over and held onto him. Christian wrapped his arms around his wife and tried his best to console her. He said nothing as he held her and listened to her sob.

Abigail's tears soaked the front of his uniform, but this didn't matter to Christian as he stroked her head and tried to calm her. Abigail clung onto Christian with desperation, like a frightened child would cling to her mother. After a moment she loosened her tight grip, and Christian peered deep into her apprehensive blue eyes. He soothed her soul by saying he loved her in a soft, gentle voice.

After hearing his son's news, it didn't take long for Ian to return home. He cleared his work schedule for the rest of the day so he could spend time with his son and Christian. Isabelle also made it home rather fast, as she had also canceled all of her remaining appointments for the day.

Isabelle suggested, since it was so sizzling hot outside, they spend the rest of the day at the beach. She and Abigail packed a picnic lunch, the men packed up chairs and a large beach umbrella, and by eleven they were headed for the cool waters they hoped would wash away the sadness clinging to them like the hot, sticky humidity. The temperature was headed toward the century mark, and the unforgiving, relentless August sun scorched the earth beneath their feet.

The five of them frolicked at the beach until five, when they all decided it was time to head home. Isabelle suggested they pick up some Chinese food for dinner because she wasn't in the mood to cook. Everyone thought this was a fantastic proposal, and it would cut down on cleanup afterwards, too.

The clock seemed to spin at a fast, brutal, unfair rate on this day. Tomorrow at this time, Christian and Alexander would be on their way to a foreign land, leaving behind the ones they loved for one whole year. But at least they would have each other to remind them of home.

After they all finished their Chinese dinner, Isabelle suggested they each pick a fortune cookie and read aloud the message.

"I'll go first," Abigail said, picking one of the cookies from the center of the table and cracking it open. She unfolded the message, cleared her throat, and read: "The secret you guard will soon come to pass." Abigail squirmed a little in her chair as she locked eyes with Alexander, the only one in the family who knew her secret.

"I suppose I can go next," Isabelle said. She opened her cookie and read: "What you are about to give will one day return home safe."

Ian read next: "What you are losing can never be lost."

Christian did an eeny meeny miney moe with the two remaining cookies. He settled on the one to his left and pretended to crack it open like an egg. He pulled out the little slip of paper and read: "The seeds you have planted will grow in your absence." Upon hearing this fortune, Abigail almost fell out of her chair.

Alexander opened the only remaining fortune cookie and stared at its contents. Instead of reading it from the slip of paper, he slid it into his pocket, then spoke: "Mine said, you will find love when love finds you."

Abigail saw right through her brother's feeble attempt to lie, but no one else seemed to notice. She pretended not to catch on… at least for now.

"Well, those were some interesting and vague fortunes," Isabelle said as she stood up and started to clean the table off.

Everyone helped tidy up the table, and soon they all moved into the living room to spend the rest of the evening just relaxing in each other's pleasant company.

Ian and Isabelle took turns telling stories, about being kids themselves and about their own children. Some of the tales were funny, and others sad.

As the evening was winding to an end, Isabelle stood up and removed an old silver cross from her necklace. She signaled for Alexander to come over to her. "Alexander, the time has come for me to pass down this family heirloom to you. This old silver cross has been in our family for three generations, and now you are the fourth generation. It has been handed down from father to son, starting with your great-grandfather to your grandfather. Since I was an only child, my father bestowed it upon me. Now, I give it to you with all my heart. One day you can give it to your son." Isabelle handed Alexander the cross and watched, smiling as he put it onto his own chain.

Alexander was amazed at how solid and heavy the old silver cross felt. He turned it over and noticed the first names of his mother, grandfather, and great-grandfather engraved on the cross.

"I wish I would've had time to get your name engraved on there before you left tomorrow," Isabelle sighed, disappointment clinging on her words.

"It's okay, Mom. There will be plenty of time for me to engrave it when Christian and I get back home." Alexander gave his mom a long, heartfelt hug.

"Alexander, if it is okay with you, I'd like to leave a little earlier than we have to in the morning so I can say goodbye to my parents at the cemetery," Christian said.

"Okay then, let's plan to leave at eight tomorrow morning."

Christian agreed with a slight nod. Then he and Abigail said goodnight to Ian, Isabelle, and Alexander, giving them all hearty hugs full of love and appreciation. Christian took his beautiful bride by the hand and they walked upstairs to their bedroom. Abigail shut the door behind her, and this modern-day Romeo and Juliet shared a quiet, romantic evening with what little time they had remaining, together alone.

Alexander soon excused himself from his parents' company and also went up to his room. He sat down on the edge of his bed, quavering inside with fear, and reached deep into his pocket to retrieve the tiny piece of paper containing his fortune. As he read it again, his hands violently trembled. A deep feeling of angst consumed Alexander's heart as he ripped the fortune into tiny pieces and threw them in his garbage can. He got down on his knees, and prayed to God for strength.

Alexander cried as he finished his prayers. Then he stood up, turned off the lights, and crawled into bed, wishing he would die in his sleep.

Chapter 15

VALEDICTION

Their bedroom, cast in a shadowy darkness, reverberated a brutal despair. Christian and Abigail couldn't slumber, terrified to know if they closed their eyes and drifted to sleep that somehow, and someway, time would cheat them out of their last remaining hours together.

Abigail was lying on her side with Christian nestled close behind her. He could hear her faint sobbing echoing throughout the darkness. With his pointer finger, he traced the words "I love you" delicately onto her back, hoping to ease her profound anguish with his gentle touch.

"Christian, can you sleep at all?" Abigail rolled over to face him.

"No. What about you?"

"No," Abigail replied.

Christian snuggled closer to her. "Eskimo kisses," he said, nuzzling his nose onto Abigail's nose. He always did Eskimo kisses when she was feeling down to make her feel better.

"Butterfly kisses," Abigail replied softly. She fluttered her long eyelashes against Christian's eyelashes and smiled, her tender heart aching with love.

"Speaking of butterflies, I have a favor to ask of you." Christian sat up and turned the bedside light on. "Will you hold onto the butterfly key my mother left for me while I'm gone? It would mean a great deal to me if you were to safeguard it with your heart." He opened the nightstand drawer, removed the key from its resting place, and handed it to her.

"I'm privileged you believe in me enough to let me hold onto this key for you." Abigail struggled to fight back the tears welling in her eyes once more.

Christian looked into his beautiful bride's beleaguered light blue eyes. The mix of tears and lack of rest was unmistakable. Abigail's eyes, now pinkish-red and puffy, needed a respite. Christian understood Abigail needed a reprieve from her crying, so he promised her he would write to her every day. This made Abigail happy inside and eased her anguish.

"Let's try to get some sleep, my love. I'll hold you tight for the rest of the night," Christian whispered. He turned off the bedside lamp and snuggled up behind her.

After they maneuvered into a comfortable position, Christian started to rub Abigail's tummy with slow, affectionate strokes. Abigail considered telling him right at that moment she was pregnant, but then decided against saying anything. Christian's incident on the tugboat and the message in her fortune cookie were the determining factors in her silence. Instead, Abigail snuggled up as close as she could get to Christian's warm body. It didn't take long for sleep to overtake her weary mind.

The abrupt, steady drone of the alarm clock roused Christian and Abigail from their shallow slumber. Christian rolled over and turned off the buzzer, grumbling aloud as he sat up in bed. Seven o'clock, only one more hour until Christian and Alexander would have to say goodbye to their families.

Christian and Abigail struggled with bleary eyes and worn-out minds after just a few hours of restless sleep. Christian dressed in his neat, pressed army uniform, while Abigail snuck into the bathroom to take her dose of anti-nausea medication. After that, Christian and Abigail went downstairs into the kitchen and Ian, Isabelle, and Alexander greeted them.

"Planning on staying in your nightgown all day, Abigail?" Alexander asked.

"As a matter of fact, I am," Abigail replied. The grogginess cleared from her head while she yawned and stretched her arms high in the air.

"You two look like death warmed over," Ian said to Christian and Abigail.

"We didn't get much sleep, and what little rest we did get wasn't of any quality," Abigail said. She rubbed her eyes in vain, too exhausted mentally and physically to wake up.

"Would any of you care for any breakfast this morning?" Isabelle asked, putting on her apron.

"I'll take a little of whatever you make," Christian replied.

Abigail's stomach churned. "Not me. I'll wait until Christian and Alexander leave." She sat down at the table and waited for her medication to kick in and quell the faint feeling of nausea rolling around inside of her tummy.

Not many words broke the eerie silence in the kitchen this morning. The clock on the wall continued to move with monotonous ticks, counting down every second until deployment. Like an approaching train, eight o'clock was coming and no one could stop it.

"Five-minute warning, Christian," Alexander said, somberness clinging to his words.

Christian and Alexander, impeccably dressed in their army uniforms, picked up their heavy army duffle bags, slung them across their broad shoulders, and headed outside. Ian, Isabelle, and Abigail followed them out the door. The morning heat and heavy humidity greeted them all with harsh slaps across their faces.

The five of them walked down the porch steps and cobblestone sidewalk to Christian's truck. The young men tossed their weighty duffle bags into the back of the vehicle and turned toward Ian, Isabelle, and Abigail. Ian and Isabelle hugged Christian first, while Abigail hugged her brother.

"What did your fortune cookie really say, Alexander?" Abigail asked, whispering in his ear while they hugged.

Alexander whispered into his sister's ear, "I can't tell you. Some things are just better kept a secret. Wouldn't you agree?"

"I suppose you're right," she whispered back.

After a few minutes, Alexander and Christian switched places. Ian and Isabelle embraced their only son with all the affection their hearts could give. He hugged them back, absorbing their love and listening to both of them cry.

Abigail couldn't hold her tears back any longer. When Christian put his arms around her, she quit fighting the sorrow and let the floodgates open. Tears streamed down her cheeks like a swollen river's floodwaters bursting through its reinforced levee.

Christian knew any words he spoke to Abigail would be fruitless. Instead, he just held her in his arms, whispering the words "I love you" over and over into her ear. His hands massaged her, the left caressing the small of her back and the right stroking the back of her neck and head with a gentle tenderness.

Ian, Isabelle, and Alexander watched Abigail buckle under the weight of her sadness as Christian held her in his arms.

Alexander looked down at his watch: eight o'clock now. He placed his hand on Christian's shoulder and whispered, "I'm sorry Christian. It's time to leave."

"No, no, no!" Abigail cried out, weeping.

Christian couldn't get Abigail to release her tense grasp on his waist, so he placed his hands onto her cheeks and wiped away the tears that fell from her red, swollen eyes. Abigail's moist cheeks glistened in the morning sun as he looked deep into her eyes and softly shushed her. For just a fleeting moment of time, her tears stopped flowing.

Christian leaned forward and pressed his lips onto her delicate lips. Without a doubt, this was the purest, sweetest, most innocent kiss of true love he had ever given Abigail. His kiss echoed a deep, devoted, everlasting love for her and, like an earthquake, shook her soul to the core. The ensuing aftershocks of his kiss would continue to resonate in the long, lonely, difficult months ahead. Christian's kiss forever imprinted on Abigail's tender heart, strong mind, and precious soul a precise balance of love that made Abigail's spirit find peace.

Ian and Isabelle pulled Abigail away from Christian. She turned and buried her head into her mother's chest, while her father held her from behind. Abigail couldn't bear to watch her husband and brother as they jumped into Christian's truck and drove out of sight.

Ian and Isabelle walked their daughter into the house. Abigail and her dad sat down at the antique dining room table. Isabelle went into the kitchen and whipped up some breakfast for Abigail.

"Abigail, dear, try to eat some of these eggs. Or have some toast, or sausage and hash browns," Isabelle said. She set the plate of food in front of Abigail, then sat down between her husband and daughter.

Abigail picked up her fork and took a bite. The nausea medication had settled her tummy. She took another bite, and then another. Before long, Abigail was shoveling food in her mouth, devouring it at a breakneck speed. Ian and Isabelle watched, amazed as their petite daughter stuffed her mouth like a suitcase.

"Abigail, slow down or you'll choke," Isabelle said.

"Yeah, what are you doing, eating for two?" Ian joked.

Abigail stopped eating and stared at her parents with a childish look of guilt, as if she were four years old and had just been busted for finger-painting on the wall.

Ian and Isabelle looked at one another and asked at the same time, "Are you pregnant?"

Abigail swallowed the last bit of food in her mouth and whispered, "Yes."

Ian and Isabelle fell over themselves as they tried to get out of their chairs to congratulate their daughter with warm embraces.

"Mom and Dad, Christian doesn't know I'm pregnant, and he won't know until he returns home," Abigail said, her tone decisive.

Both Ian and Isabelle looked at one another and frowned. "Why didn't you tell him?" they asked in unison.

Abigail took a deep breath and explained her reasons to them. She made her parents promise to keep her pregnancy a secret, and they pledged that they would, even though they didn't agree with her decision.

* * *

Christian parked his truck in the cemetery and left it running so Alexander could enjoy the comfort of the ice-cold air conditioning.

"Alexander, give me five minutes, please," Christian said, stepping out of his truck. He made his way to his parents' graves and sat down on the wooden bench. After a few minutes of silence, he spoke. "I wanted to let you both know I won't be around for a while. Alexander and I are on our way to Afghanistan, deploying for a one-year tour of duty. I know this will sound selfish, but I'll ask anyway. Could you two please watch over Abigail for me? She's taking all this rather hard, and I'd be appreciative if you'd just be there for her while I'm away."

Christian looked around for a sign of acknowledgement but saw nothing. However, there are miraculous things in life you sometimes just cannot see with the naked eye. Christian's parents were present, and they stood resplendent behind him. Noah and Elizabeth each placed a translucent hand onto Christian's shoulders while he sat on the faded wooden bench. Upon their touch, Christian's eyes fluttered, like butterfly wings in flight, and a wave of peace swept over his soul. All the fears he carried in his heart disappeared and his spirit became calm and light. A wondrous feeling that all would be well at home in his long absence swept over him.

Slowly, Noah and Elizabeth withdrew their hands from Christian's shoulders, and his eyes stopped fluttering. He jumped up and spun around to behold... nothing. The hair on his neck stood on end. He paused for a moment to absorb the miraculous experience.

Christian glanced at his watch and realized he was running behind schedule, so he sprinted to his truck and hopped into the driver's seat. As Christian sped out of the cemetery, Alexander held on for dear life.

Silently, with sadness in their hearts, Noah and Elizabeth stood on their consecrated ground, and watched their son leave for war.

* * *

Christian and Alexander made it to Colonel Andrews' office with two minutes to spare. They set their military duffle bags on the floor outside the office and knocked on the door.

"You may enter," Colonel Andrews called out with a loud, firm voice.

Both young men walked into his office and stood at attention in front of his desk.

"At ease, gentlemen, and plant your butts into those chairs again," the Colonel commanded. "Lieutenant Kabecka will be here soon."

"Sir... permission to speak freely?" Christian asked.

Colonel Andrews focused his eyes on Christian, then nodded. "Permission granted, Specialist Bryson."

"Is Lieutenant Kabecka new to the unit, sir?"

"Yes, he just transferred in from the previous unit that was guarding the road block and checkpoint that we're now assigned to guard. This will be his second tour of duty over in Afghanistan. On a side note, gentlemen, I know how you enlisted men love to mess around with the new officers, but please cut Lieutenant Kabecka some slack. You didn't hear this from me, but three weeks ago, his twin brother, who was also a lieutenant, was shot and killed in action at the same checkpoint we are now protecting."

Christian and Alexander nodded, showing that they understood.

Soon Lieutenant Kabecka entered the office. His frame was short and stocky. He had coal-black hair, and his shadowy, silvery-grey eyes made a ghostly impression. His dark complexion made it easy to tell he was of Native American origin, most likely the Ojibwa tribe, Christian and Alexander guessed.

Lieutenant Kabecka gave Christian and Alexander the once over, his eyes twinkling as he spoke. "Specialist Bryson, Specialist Havily, it's time to deploy. I have procured our military flight to Afghanistan. Gentlemen, let's move!"

"Yes, sir," Christian and Alexander replied. They stood up and quickly followed the Lieutenant, off to war.

Chapter 16

SHOEBOX LOVE LETTERS

The long, hot, humid dog days of summer had come and gone, as had the vivid, beautiful autumn, with the oak trees' leaves shifting color like a chameleon's skin. As the bitter cold of winter started to set in, the birds began their annual retreat to the warm, inviting states to the south. Christmas came and went as Ian, Isabelle, and Abigail shared their gifts with one another, storing Alexander and Christian's presents for when they returned home. The brutal winter and the thick, white blanket of snow that covered everything soon gave way to the warm late-March rays of sunlight and the milder days of spring. Life had returned to the once-frozen tundra. The birds arrived back from their long migration, and the trees began to show signs of color.

Abigail was almost full term, and her once-petite frame, now gravid and swollen, ached with a throbbing wonderfulness. Her ankles and feet swelled, and her bellybutton protruded from her tummy, jutting out like a meat thermometer on an overcooked roast. When she walked, her entire body wobbled, like a penguin trying to waddle in an earthquake.

Over the months Abigail's resolve had grown tough. She displayed a gritty fortitude as she made her way to the wooden mailbox at the end of the long driveway. She had inherited her mother's strong determination and iron will, and refused to wait for her parents to bring her Christian's letters from the mailbox. She walked out and got them herself. It didn't matter one bit if the weather rained, snowed, hailed, sleeted, thundered, or blew. Abigail thumbed her nose at Mother Nature's mood swings and made her daily pilgrimage to the mailbox to meet Evangeline, her mail carrier. Evangeline usually stayed and talked with Abigail for a few minutes, checking on the progress of her pregnancy and catching up on how Christian was doing.

Abigail received a love letter almost every day from Christian. Sometimes she received two letters, usually on a Monday. The forty-eight hour stretch from Saturday to Monday, when mail delivery resumed, proved difficult for Abigail, and on Mondays, she waited, anxious for Evangeline to arrive with Christian's charming correspondences.

This day, Abigail didn't have to wait long for Evangeline to show up in her mail truck. Evangeline greeted her with a smile. "Good afternoon, Abigail. It looks like you have two letters today."

"Two?" This surprised Abigail. Today was Friday, not Monday.

"Yes ma'am, you have two, although it appears one is from your brother." Evangeline handed over the letters and some other mail.

"Thank you, Evangeline." Abigail eyes beamed with joy at the anticipation of reading the love letter from her husband.

"You're very welcome, dear. It won't be long now until you're a mommy," Evangeline stated with enthusiasm.

"Sorry, I've got to run now. I wish I could talk longer but I'm a little behind on my route."

Abigail bid farewell to Evangeline and looked down at today's treasure. She thought of each letter as a cherished jewel, and when she opened it, she treated every engaging word that Christian wrote as if it were a precious gem. The beautiful words he wrote filled her heart and soul with an astounding love.

She turned and wobbled back up the long driveway, smiling as the sun's warm rays kissed her cheeks. The afternoon was wonderful, a perfect spring day for being alive and outside. Not too hot, not too cold. Just right. Abigail enjoyed the fresh air and the sounds of robins singing to one another. When she reached the porch, she decided to stay outside to enjoy the inviting ambience and the surrounding sounds of nature.

Abigail sat down on the porch swing, resting her aching back and swollen feet. She opened the envelope from Alexander first and found a small note and a second letter addressed to their father inside. The note to Abigail instructed her to give the letter to their dad only in the event of a catastrophe. An uneasy feeling swept over Abigail, and her stomach sank as if she were riding on a roller coaster. What did her brother's ominous words hold? She put Alexander's unnerving letter aside.

Abigail needed something more positive, and Christian's letter was just the dose of medication to lift her spirits high. With the utmost care, she opened Christian's envelope and then read his romantic words three times over. His careful penmanship and exquisite words brought pleasure to Abigail's spirit, like premium chocolate chunk ice cream to her taste buds. She savored every word, just like she did with every scrumptious, delectable mouth-watering bite of her frozen delight. Abigail sighed deeply as she pressed Christian's letter up to her chest and thought of the last kiss they shared on that hot August morning before his deployment.

Abigail's eyes had grown heavy; the later stages of her pregnancy sapped her body. The growing progeny inside her demanded more of her energy. She rose from the porch swing and eased herself up in a slow, careful motion. She picked up Christian and Alexander's letters along with the other mail, then wobbled inside, detouring to the dining room to place the rest of the mail on the table for her parents.

Upstairs, in her bedroom, Abigail sat down on her bed and reached for one of the five shoeboxes on the nightstand. Each one was filled with Christian's correspondences. She filed his most recent letter behind the others, keeping them in chronological order. Abigail smiled. Her heart was content and her eyes twinkled. She gazed upon her collection of nearly two-hundred and fifty love letters from Christian. In another few weeks, she would need to start another shoebox.

Abigail yawned and stretched, then rested her drowsy head on her pillow filled with eiderdown. As she lay flat on her back, she caressed her outsized stomach and sang a sweet lullaby to the precious, always-growing seed that Christian had planted inside her. She pulled the soft comforter over herself, closed her eyes, and drifted off to sleep. Abigail dreamed of reading the next romantic love letter that Christian would pen.

Chapter 17

THE ENIGMA

One thing that made life bearable for Christian was being able to share a small room on base with Alexander, just the two of them.

The secret base, located deep inside the mountains, stood fortified by the earth's natural barricade. Just outside the entrance to the secret base, about fifty yards away and strategically placed in a tight gorge between two mountains, sat the checkpoint and roadblock that Christian and Alexander guarded every day. The checkpoint safeguarded the only entrance to the secret mountain installation. Everything and everyone had to come through that checkpoint to reach the mountain hideaway, which made the duty of guarding it important and perilous. To date, thirteen enlisted men and two officers had sacrificed their lives for their country while protecting this barren, inhospitable piece of real estate.

Inside their small quarters, Christian and Alexander played cribbage as they waited for their shift to begin in less than an hour. Their room's sparse contents included one bunk bed, one small table with two chairs, one small desk with a single rolling chair, and a clock on the wall. A soft knock on the door interrupted their game.

"You can come in. It's unlocked," Christian called out, playing the five of hearts and announcing "15-2."

"Good morning, gentleman," Lieutenant Kabecka said, entering the room. "Ah cribbage. I love that game."

"Care to join us, sir?" Alexander asked.

"No thanks, gentleman. I'm just here to check on you both."

Christian and Alexander respected Lieutenant Kabecka. He cared for his men's wellbeing and acted like a shepherd overseeing and protecting his flock. He was a people person, just like Colonel Andrews.

"I hope everything's fine and that this unpleasant duty isn't wearing on your morale," Lieutenant Kabecka said.

"We're fine, sir. Thanks for asking," Christian replied.

"Is there anything you want that I could requisition for you?"

"There is something I'd like to know, but it may be none of my business, sir," Alexander said.

"What's your question, Specialist Havily?"

Alexander took a deep breath. "Well, sir, please forgive me if I'm out of line. The other night while I was praying, the thought of your twin brother crossed my mind. I have a twin sister myself and Christian is married to her. I was wondering if you'd be willing to tell us more about him and what it's like to lose a sibling."

Lieutenant Kabecka looked down at his watch and decided he had a little time, so he pulled the desk chair up to the table and sat down. He looked at Christian and Alexander for a moment, mulling over the right words to say.

"Losing a sibling is indescribable. It's worse than losing a good friend. I've lost both, so believe me when I tell you that. And when you have a twin, a womb mate, a mirror image of yourself, you have a unique and special bond that no one else can understand. When your twin dies, a large part of you dies, too. There's no other way I can explain it." Lieutenant Kabecka tightened his lips, trying to mask his sorrow.

"What was your brother's name?" Alexander asked.

"How about I tell you some of my family heritage first? Then I'll come back to our names."

Alexander nodded. "That sounds good to me."

"My brother and I were born into a very poor family on the reservation. Our last name, Kabecka, means twins. When my mother gave birth, my brother came first in the bright daylight hours of the summer. Butterflies fluttered all around our father and mother as my brother entered this world, so my father named him Memengwa, which translates to butterfly. I, on the other hand, proved a little more stubborn. My mother struggled to push me out, but I refused to see the light of day. Finally, after night settled in, I entered this world surrounded by fireflies that illuminated the dark sky with a dazzling radiance, so my father named me Wonyecha, which translates to firefly. My mother, like yours, Christian, died soon after childbirth."

"How did you know about my mother's death?" Christian asked, mystified.

Lieutenant Kabecka didn't answer Christian. He glanced at his watch, stood up, and walked to the door. Before he left, he turned around and looked at Christian and Alexander. He flashed them a smile, and his silver-gray eyes twinkled as he spoke. "I'll see you gentleman at the checkpoint in thirty minutes." Lieutenant Kabecka turned and went out the door. Christian and Alexander were intrigued, not only by the Lieutenant's final statement to Christian but also by the aura around him. He seemed like a man wrapped in silent riddles.

"Well, that was interesting," Alexander stated. He stood up and stretched.

"Yeah, I agree. I suppose we'd better straighten up the room and get ready for guard duty."

The two young men quickly cleaned up their quarters, then dressed in their fatigues. A silent nod between them said they were ready to go, and with that, they went out the door for duty.

* * *

Because the checkpoint was wedged so tightly between two mountainside cliffs, the soldiers had dubbed it the "chokepoint." The only way anyone could get through the bottleneck and close to the secret installation was through the one officer and ten enlisted men who guarded it with their lives.

At eighteen-hundred hours, Christian and Alexander were halfway through their twelve-hour guard shift. Lieutenant Kabecka had assigned Alexander to the radio station inside the guardhouse, and Christian's assignment was to check in vehicles that approached the checkpoint. Christian stationed himself fifteen yards out from the guardhouse. The other eight Red Bulls were operating two machine gun nests on either side of the checkpoint, abutting the walls of the mountains.

The evening was shaping up as yet another boring, monotonous shift. The weather, decent for the most part, had stayed warm with temperatures that hovered around seventy-five degrees. The blue sky contained large, puffy, white clouds that at times blocked out the sun's warm rays.

Alexander waved through the guardhouse window, letting Christian know that he would be out to relieve him in five minutes. Christian waved back in acknowledgement. As Alexander and Lieutenant Kabecka were enjoying a piping hot cup of coffee, disaster struck.

Rocks and debris rained down from the mountainside as rocket-propelled grenades scored direct hits on both machine gun nests, killing the eight Red Bulls stationed there. The repercussions from the simultaneous explosions sent shockwaves though the guardhouse, which collapsed around Alexander and Lieutenant Kabecka. The Lieutenant was trapped under the rubble, but Alexander, shielded from the brunt of the explosion by the radio desk, was free.

"Help me, Havily," the Lieutenant pleaded, trying in vain to free himself from the debris piled on top of him.

Christian, unprotected during the blast, lay face down on the rocky ground, broken and bloodied. Alexander could see him lying motionless, exposed to any snipers who were lurking and looking for an easy kill.

Alexander now stood at a crossroads in the path of his short life. What he chose would ultimately be his defining moment and the turning point for two lives that could be either lost or saved. He had two choices: leave the Lieutenant and rush out to save Christian, or free the Lieutenant before another grenade hit what was left of the guardhouse and leave Christian exposed to sniper fire.

Alexander wanted to charge out to Christian's aid, but he couldn't force himself to do that first. The Lieutenant was alive for sure, he reasoned, and Christian might not be. Alexander frantically pulled what rubble he could off Lieutenant Kabecka, then grabbed him by his arms and yanked him out. The Lieutenant screamed in agony as Alexander dragged him to the safety of reinforced sandbags. Just as Alexander shoved the Lieutenant over the sandbag embankment, another rocket-propelled grenade slammed into the remnants of the guardhouse. Shrapnel ripped into Alexander's legs and back, knocking him to his knees.

"Get your butt undercover, Havily. That's an order!" Lieutenant Kabecka commanded.

"I'm sorry, sir, but I'll never be able to look my sister in the eye or live with myself if I just let Christian die!" Alexander turned and tried to run to his fallen friend, but Lieutenant Kabecka held him back.

"He's already dead, Alexander!" Lieutenant Kabecka continued his stranglehold on Alexander's arm, and prevented him from rushing out into the line of fire.

Alexander turned toward the Lieutenant, who had never called him by his first name before. The two men locked eyes, and a wave of destiny swept over Alexander as a flash of white light reflected off Lieutenant Kabecka's ghostly eyes.

"I'm sorry, sir. I won't obey that order even if you're God himself!" Alexander clenched his right hand into a fist and punched the Lieutenant square in the nose. The Lieutenant fell, out cold. Or was he?

Alexander kissed the silver cross his mother had given him, said a quick prayer for protection, and headed for Christian. Alexander was losing blood rapidly, but his injuries couldn't stop him. They could only slow him down on the path to his destiny.

The sniper had Alexander in his crosshairs, and a sudden, earsplitting shot rang out, echoing off the mountains walls. The sniper's piercing bullet tore into Alexander's shoulder with devastating force, knocking him down just a few feet away from Christian. Blood gushed from his new wound, and Alexander grew more and more lightheaded as he crawled to Christian, frantic to reach him in time.

In a few seconds, Alexander reached Christian and he instinctively threw his bloodied body over his friend, shielding him from the sniper's determined fire. Tears of pain and fear washed over Alexander's face. "You have to live, Christian. Your family is going to need you," he whispered, his strength fading fast.

The sound of a second shot reverberated off the mountain walls. The sniper's bullet ripped into the back of Alexander's neck with devastating force, and severed the chain holding the silver cross. The cross fell to the earth, beside the two young men who lay motionless on the hard, rocky ground.

An eerie calm lingered in the mountain air. Scattered among the carnage were the bodies of the good men who had given their lives for their country and one another.

Chapter 18

AMBIGUITY

A warm, gentle breeze blew through the town of Columbus this afternoon, circulating the air with a breath of new life. Saturday: a day of rest in the Havily household, but not today. Ian and Isabelle decided to go outside and make plans for planting their springtime flower garden. While they debated whether they should add another rose bush or two to their garden, they heard a car approaching the house.

They turned to see their visitors, but their happy smiles vanished when they saw a black Cadillac coming up the driveway. Isabelle reached for her husband's hand and grasped it tight. A sick feeling overcame them as they spotted the flags on either side of the car's hood, a small U.S. flag on one side and a small Army National Guard flag of the Red Bulls on the other. Isabelle's eyes filled with tears and her body shook, her worst fears becoming a reality. Ian put his arm around his wife and squeezed her to let her know he was there for her. Their eyes never wavered off the Cadillac.

When the car came to a stop and Colonel Andrews and an army chaplain got out, Isabelle's lips quivered and she fell to her knees, trembling with a terrible fear. Ian's knees knocked, but he remained on his feet, barely, desperate to stand strong for his wife. He put his hand on Isabelle's head, trying in vain to give her strength.

Colonel Andrews stopped a few feet away from Ian and Isabelle and stood at attention. He spoke in a firm, clear voice. "Mr. and Mrs. Havily, on behalf of the United States Army, I regret to inform you of the death of your son, Alexander… and also the death of your son-in-law, Christian."

Ian closed his eyes, then fell to his knees next to Isabelle, his head hanging low. They embraced each other, both sobbing, inconsolable.

"I don't have many details on what happened over there, Mr. and Mrs. Havily, but as soon as I find out more information, you'll be notified at once." Colonel Andrews pressed his lips together and fought back the urge to cry himself. This by far was the worst day of his long, illustrious career.

The army chaplain got down onto his knees with Ian and Isabelle and started to say the Lord's Prayer. Colonel Andrews rested his hands on Ian and Isabelle's shoulders and joined in saying the prayer.

* * *

Abigail sat up and yawned as she awoke from her daily nap. She slid out of bed and put her slippers on, then waddled over to the window and opened the wood blinds to let the sun's warm rays kiss her face. She gazed outside, and the look on her face turned from bliss to horror in the blink of an eye. She witnessed Colonel Andrews and the army chaplain trying to console her grieving parents.

Abigail let out a bloodcurdling scream. She ran down the stairs, out the front door, and down the porch steps to her parents' side, tears streaming down her face.

Ian and Isabelle quickly stood up when they heard Abigail burst through the door. When she reached them, they both spread their arms and clutched her tight, knowing that the devastating news of both Christian and Alexander's premature deaths would break her heart.

"Oh my God, which one is it?" Abigail asked her parents, terrified.

Ian put his soft hands on his daughter's cheeks and looked into her eyes, knowing the words he was about to speak would cut deep, like a dagger to her heart. "It's both of them, Abigail, both of them." Ian pulled his daughter into his arms and held her, trying to extinguish the pain that burned her soul like flames.

"No, no, no!" Abigail pulled herself violently away from her dad, her face ashen and sick. She wobbled backwards, put her shaky hands on her big stomach, and looked at her parents in panic as her water broke and spilled onto the sidewalk like water running from a spigot. Abigail's eyes rolled back in her head. She fainted. Ian, Colonel Andrews, and the army chaplain all rushed to catch her before she could fall to the ground.

"We need to get her to the hospital!" Ian shouted, cradling his unconscious daughter in his arms.

"Get her into the back seat of the Cadillac. I'll drive us there!" the chaplain yelled as he rushed to the car.

Colonel Andrews put his arm around Isabelle and escorted her to the car in a frantic rush. When she, Ian, and Abigail were safely in the back seat, he slammed the door shut and jumped into the passenger seat.

"Drive!" he ordered the chaplain.

Five people who had been mourning the loss of two lives just moments before now sped to the hospital to bring new life into the world.

* * *

Abigail lay inconsolable in her hospital bed as the nurse prepared her for delivery. Soon, she would be moved to the hospital's birthing ward. Isabelle would accompany Abigail and be her birthing partner in lieu of Christian. Outside of the room, Colonel Andrews and the army chaplain did their best to console Ian.

Abigail cried in gasping shudders. "Mom, I can't do this without Christian. I don't want to do it without him."

"Abigail, you can't think about Christian now. It's time to think about yourself and the special package you carry inside you. Christian would want you to continue your life, to give birth." Isabelle tried to remain strong for her daughter in her moment of need.

Colonel Andrews tightened his lips. "I'm sorry, Mr. Havily, for the loss of your son and your son-in-law. I know my words can't take away your anguish, but if there is anything I can do to ease your mind and heart, please let me know."

"There is something you can do," Ian said. "Our family will need closure. Please find out what happened and how they died."

Colonel Andrews nodded. As he put his hand on Ian's shoulder, one of the two cell phones he carried rang out, the one used to contact him in an emergency. "Excuse me for a moment, Mr. Havily. I need to take this call."

The Colonel walked a few feet away and answered: "This is Colonel Andrews and this better be important." He had left explicit orders that he not be interrupted during this difficult official visit with the Havily family. The Colonel listened intently and a long pause ensued. "Are you one hundred percent sure?" Another long pause. "All right then, I understand. Call me back if you find out any more details." The Colonel walked back to Ian and stood before him, a peculiar look on his face.

Ian looked at Colonel Andrews and sensed something out of the ordinary. "What's wrong?" he asked.

"Mr. Havily, on behalf of the United States Army, I am pleased to inform you that your son-in-law Christian is alive. I apologize for the misinformation. Christian is in stable condition, and as we speak, a military plane is transporting him to a military hospital in Germany."

Ian couldn't believe his ears! "Abigail," Ian whispered to himself. He rushed into Abigail's room and past the scolding nurse attending to his daughter. Abigail needed to hear this miraculous news, and now, not later. No one was going to deny him from seeing her.

His eyes locked onto his sobbing daughter. This poor girl had endured so much sorrow in her short life with Christian. She deserved happiness, and he was going to deliver a message of good news for once. Ian went over to his daughter and sat on the edge of her bed. He cupped her tear-soaked cheeks in his hands, tenderness in his touch, and stared deep into her red, puffy eyes.

"What is it, Daddy?" Abigail sensed in her father's twinkling eyes that he had something amazing to say.

"It's time to make your husband a daddy. He needs to come home to his beautiful family."

Abigail replied through her sobs, "Christian will never see his family. He's dead. He's coming home in a box."

"You're wrong. Christian is alive! I just received the news from Colonel Andrews. Christian is alive! He's coming home to you, and not in a box!"

Abigail couldn't believe the good news! Neither could Isabelle, who rushed over for a long family hug.

"What about Alexander?" Abigail asked.

The happiness left Ian's face as fast as it had come, replaced by the sad realization of his son's death.

Ian hung his head low. "No, Abigail. Alexander is dead."

Her heart sank like a brick in water. "I'm so sorry, Daddy." Abigail looked to him with tear-filled eyes. "And Mom." She reached for Isabelle's hand.

Ian hardened himself. "Abigail, you need to focus on the task ahead, and that's to give birth to the special package you've carried for almost nine months. It's time for you and Christian to become parents. Your mother and I are ready to become grandparents, too!"

Her father had always been an inspiration to Abigail, and after hearing his words, her resolve hardened like mortar to brick. She was ready to face the arduous task ahead, to deliver the progeny who would be loved unconditionally, with unparalleled devotion.

"Thank you, Daddy," Abigail said softly.

Ian gave his daughter's hands a squeeze and turned to leave. Just before he went through the door, he turned, told her he loved her, and then flashed her a smile. Ian's eyes, however, betrayed the sorrow that was mixed with his joy. Grief escaped through the windows of his besieged soul, giving Abigail a faint glimpse of her father's struggles.

In the families' waiting room, Ian sat alone with his thoughts. He was exhausted after the day's emotional ups and downs and his own battle with God's so-called providence. He put his hands over his beleaguered face, shutting out the hard world, and broke down. The realization had hit him hard, like a runaway locomotive. His son was coming home, lifeless in a box.

Chapter 19

AWAKENING INTO THE NIGHTMARE

Christian awoke with a frantic jerk. He had no idea where he was or how he had gotten there. He screamed for help and tried, without success, to sit up. The doctor and nurse rushed into the hospital room, happy to see that their patient was conscious.

"Hello, son. My name is Major Kavanagh, and I'm your physician. Can you tell me your name?"

"Specialist Christian Bryson, attached to the 34th Red Bulls from Minnesota. Sir, where am I? What happened to me? I can't remember a thing."

"Take it easy, son," Major Kavanagh said, his voice calm and soothing. "You're in the hospital on a U.S. Army base in Germany. You've been unconscious for the better part of three days. What's the last thing you remember?"

Christian struggled to think, his mind still short-circuited from the explosion that rendered him unconscious. "I was…" He paused to concentrate. "I was standing guard duty and a huge explosion went off… Oh my God, where's Alexander? Where's Specialist Havily?" Christian's mind raced as panic overtook him.

"I'm sorry, Specialist Bryson. I don't know, but I can tell you something about what happened. The checkpoint you were guarding was hit by rocket-launched grenades, and an explosion knocked you unconscious. In surgery, we removed shrapnel from the front side of your body—from the ankles all the way up to your neck. You're lucky. You could've died."

Christian looked down with hesitance to see if he still had all of his limbs. He wiggled his fingers and toes, then breathed a sigh of relief that all were still in place.

"Specialist Bryson, I'm afraid there is some bad news to relay to you. One piece of shrapnel severed..." Major Kavanagh paused to find the correct words. "Son, you can still make love to your wife, but you won't be able to father children."

This news devastated Christian. He'd promised Abigail a family. Now he couldn't give Abigail what she wanted most: children.

"The rest of your wounds were superficial and are healing well, so we've set up a military flight to move you back home to the Twin Cities. You'll spend a night or two in the VA hospital and then be released back to your guard unit, probably to desk duty."

Major Kavanagh and the nurse left the room, leaving Christian all alone with his thoughts. As he lay in the silence of his hospital room, Christian sank deeper and deeper into the inner abyss of depression. He closed his eyes and faded off to sleep, hoping to either awaken from this cruel nightmare or die in his sleep.

* * *

The three days after Ian and Isabelle learned of their son's death had been filled with sorrow and mourning, but they had been wondrous days, too. They'd become grandparents, and this helped fill the empty void in their broken hearts.

Abigail wrestled with her emotions, going from extreme happiness that Christian was alive to profound sadness that her brother was dead. She wanted to know what had happened to Alexander, and also Christian. Exhausted, Abigail turned on the baby monitor and decided to take a nap.

In Stillwater, Minnesota, Colonel Andrews stood in somber silence with Ian and Isabelle at the headquarters of the Red Bulls. Together, the three waited for the military truck carrying Alexander's remains to arrive from the airport. Alexander's casket, patriotically draped with the U.S. flag, arrived with no fanfare and no hero's welcome. Isabelle sobbed as she watched military personnel move her son's flag-draped casket from the military truck to an awaiting hearse.

The precious life Ian and Isabelle had created together was gone, cruelly snatched from this world. No longer would they hear their son's beautiful voice or feel the warmth and love in his tender hugs. Loss and emptiness filled Ian and Isabelle, like someone had taken an eraser and wiped clean the chalkboard that was Alexander's life. But their memories of him could never be erased. They would forever cherish his undying spirit, and the many recollections of Alexander's laugh, his smile, and his affection would help Ian and Isabelle make it through each grueling day without him.

"I've gotten some details from Lieutenant Kabecka about your son's death," Colonel Andrews said once the hearse was out of sight. "Alexander impetuously rushed out to Christian's aid from his safe position, even though he had grievous wounds to his back and legs. He threw himself on top of Christian's body, and saved your son-in-law's life by taking the sniper bullets meant for him. Lieutenant Kabecka has submitted your son's heroic deeds for the Medal of Honor."

Ian and Isabelle were proud and surprised by the information, and they thanked the Colonel for telling them. However, the news did not sit well with Ian.

Ian struggled to understand his son's actions. He couldn't accept the idea that Alexander had sacrificed his life for Christian's life. He started to second-guess Abigail's decision to tell Alexander, but not Christian, that she was pregnant. Would Alexander have given his life if he hadn't known about Abigail's pregnancy? A tug-of-war wrenched Ian's mind back and forth, and he fought against blaming his daughter for her indirect influence in Alexander's fatal decision to save Christian.

At home, Ian and Isabelle made preparations for Alexander's funeral, to take place in just three days. They had opted for a closed-casket service due to the massive injuries to Alexander's body. They wanted everyone attending the funeral service to remember Alexander as he was when he was alive.

Ian sat at the antique dining room table with pen and paper, reluctantly undertaking the task of writing a beautiful eulogy for Alexander's funeral. What he wanted to say wasn't coming to him. Time ticked by, but the paper before him remained as blank as the look on his face. Ian's soul was numb and his body raw after three long days of crying. When Abigail entered the room carrying an envelope, an incongruous bitterness crept into Ian's heart. Their eyes locked and Abigail could sense something dark brewing within her father that she had never felt before.

"Dad, Alexander wanted you to have this letter if something horrible happened to him," Abigail said, her voice barely audible as she handed over the envelope.

Ian didn't say as much as thank you to his daughter. His eyes burned as he snatched the envelope from an uncomprehending Abigail.

"I'm so sorry," she said, tears filling her eyes as she put her arms around her father.

A chill radiated from Ian, like frost on a windowpane on a nippy November morning, and Abigail quickly pulled away. She was the target of his anger and bitterness, she realized. When she tried again to speak to him, he cut her off abruptly. Abigail ran upstairs to her room, heartbroken, crying the entire way.

The slow trickle of doubt in Ian's heart that started soon after Noah died had now grown to full flood stage with the death of his son. The last remnants of his once-strong faith were bleeding away. Ian would need a divine miracle to pull him out of his kamikaze dive toward the bottomless depths of Abaddon.

Ian opened the envelope from Alexander, removed the letter, and slowly read every word. Then he folded the letter with care, returned it to its envelope, buried his head in his arms on the table, and cried in great, shuddering gasps.

* * *

Isabelle, curled up on the living room couch with her blanket and a box of tissues, held a wooden box containing Alexander's personal effects. Colonel Andrews had given it to her earlier in the day, but as yet, she hadn't mustered the strength to open it. She took a deep breath, then with trembling hands, she opened the box. Inside she found Alexander's watch, wallet, dog tags, and broken necklace. The old silver cross she had given her son before he deployed was not there.

Isabelle broke down, crying miserably. The family heirloom, passed down to her from her father, was forever lost, just like her son. She placed Alexander's belongings back into the box with care, then laid her weary head on the couch, pulled the blanket over her shoulders, and cried herself to sleep.

* * *

Abigail tiptoed to the door and peeked into the nursery. She smiled and listened for a moment to the peaceful sound of quiet breathing, then gently closed the door. Without a sound, she walked into her bedroom and turned on the baby monitor that rested atop the nightstand next to her bed. She climbed into her bed, turned onto her side, and pulled the covers up over her body.

Abigail reached over and opened her nightstand drawer. She removed the elaborate, ornate butterfly key with utmost care. The key reminded her of Christian, and she held it against her heart, thinking of him close to her. Why hadn't he called yet? She struggled to ward off the overwhelming worry building up deep inside her, hoping there was a good reason. Maybe he didn't have access to a telephone. Or maybe he was too hurt to talk yet. Or maybe, just maybe, Christian didn't want to talk to anybody at all.

That thought terrified Abigail. She wanted to support her husband in his time of need. She felt powerless just lying alone in bed with no way to do anything to help. From the bits and pieces of information relayed by Colonel Andrews, Abigail knew Christian was essentially okay, but she didn't know the exact extent of his injuries, either mental or physical. She needed to talk to him. She longed to hear Christian's sweet voice, even if it was only to say hello. Just that one word would be enough to temporarily sate her yearning and allay her fear.

Abigail was exhausted, her petite body still recovering from childbirth. She looked at her alarm clock and noticed it was late, ten o'clock. She closed her eyes and prayed for Christian to call her soon. She also asked the good Lord to deliver him home safely. She thought back to the evening before Christian deployed, and her heart melted at the wonderful memory of her husband snuggled up behind her, drawing the words "I love you" on her back. Abigail smiled

at the thought of Christian's soft touch and faded off to
dreamland.

Unbeknownst to Abigail, nightmares haunted Christian's
sleep. He was neither mentally nor physically okay. He
waged war upon himself, his heart devastated by the
medical results indicating that he'd never father any
children, ever. His mind teetered on the precipice of a
breakdown, and his soul neared collapse. Christian's once-
strong heart was breaking, and he heaped contempt upon
himself for making a promise to Abigail he now could never
fulfill.

Christian awoke from a horrendous nightmare into the
new nightmare that was now his life. He sat up in his
hospital bed and looked down at his body. His legs, arms,
stomach, and chest were beginning to heal and his wounds
had started to scab over. Soreness lingered in his mid-
section but he managed to maneuver himself out of the bed
and into the chair by the telephone. He wasn't sure if it was
against the rules to make an overseas call, but he decided he
would take whatever punishment the army threw at him just
to hear Abigail's sweet voice once again. He picked up the
phone and dialed her number.

After four rings, he heard a sleepy "Hello?"

"Abigail, it's Christian."

Abigail's eyes lit up like fireworks on Independence Day
when she heard his familiar, warm voice. "Christian, talk to
me. Are you okay?"

"Yes... and no," he replied.

"What do you mean... no?" she asked, a tinge of
uncertainty creeping into her voice.

"I can't tell you yet. I'm not ready to. I can't talk long,
but I wanted you to know that sometime later in the week
I'll be coming back to the States by military transport. The
Army is moving me to the VA Hospital in the Twin Cities
for a day or two of observation. Then I'll be released."

"It's too bad you won't be home for Alexander's funeral," she said. A long, uncomfortable silence ensued. "Christian?"

"Alexander died?" Christian's stomach churned violently, like a raging whitewater rapids.

"Yes. He's dead. You didn't know?"

"No. How did..." Christian paused for a moment and collected himself. "How did he die?"

"The details are vague, but Colonel Andrews said that Alexander covered you with his body, taking two sniper bullets meant for you." Abigail's voice cracked.

This was the last straw for Christian's despondent heart. Hope gave way like an avalanche. Collapsing under the weight of the news of Alexander's death, he slumped in his chair. "I need to go now."

"No, Christian, wait! Please!" Abigail implored.

Click.

Abigail stayed on the line long after the prerecorded message began: "If you would like to make a call, please hang up and try again."

If Abigail could've foreseen any of the struggles Christian was battling, she would've told him the day he deployed about her pregnancy. But correct or not, she had made her difficult decision and now had to live with it and accept the consequences. Some paths are our destiny and, once chosen, must be followed.

Alone in her bed, sobbing, she wondered, would her husband ever call home again?

Chapter 20

ANGELS AMONG US

One and only one thing is predictable about March weather in Minnesota: it's unpredictable. Over the past few days, the sunlit skies and lukewarm temperatures had made a dramatic exit. The mercury in thermometers around town dropped when the swirling grey clouds from the cold front came rolling in from the northwest. The once-moderate temperatures plunged to below freezing and people could now see their breath in each moist exhale they made. The ice-cold humidity that accompanied the cold front chilled anyone inadequately dressed right down to the bone.

A light snow started to blow along with the wind, and the wind chill's bitter bite made the twenty degree day feel more like minus five. The weather was fit for neither man nor beast, yet two-hundred and fifty unselfish souls braved the brutal conditions to pay their final respects to Alexander and to his family.

The small church was crammed to overflowing with family and friends. In front of the altar rested Alexander's flag-draped casket, the stars on the blue field at the head, over Alexander's left shoulder, and the red and white stripes running from head to toe.

Abigail, Isabelle, and Colonel Andrews were seated in the front pew. Behind them sat close family and friends, and next were the many acquaintances Alexander had known throughout the years: neighbors, schoolteachers, coaches, and military friends.

Ian stood behind the altar, preparing to deliver the most difficult funeral service in his long, devoted career as a priest. He put on a brave face for everyone attending the ceremony, but deep inside, hidden from everyone but himself and the Lord, was the true feeling that raged inside his wounded heart: anger.

Ian was bitter, furious with God for the loss of his son. No one, including Isabelle, knew he had decided this would be the last funeral service he would ever conduct. He was quitting the priesthood after today. He no longer believed in God. Ian was lost in misery, like a ship tossing in stormy seas. He needed a miracle, a strong lighthouse beacon, to guide his misplaced soul back home to God. Without that miracle, Ian would continue to flounder in despair, lost in a lonely existence without the providence of God.

"Abigail, did you tell the babysitter you wouldn't be home until later this afternoon?" Isabelle whispered to her daughter.

"Yes, Mom. Everything has been taken care of," Abigail whispered back, a faint, forced smile parting her lips.

Ian opened the bible his daughter had given to him for his birthday many years ago. He cleared his throat, then welcomed and thanked everyone for attending the service.

"I can see with my eyes and feel with my heart that my son had many friends," Ian began. "This makes me happy, and my broken heart appreciates your support in our family's tragic time of need. I'd like to start today's service a little differently from the traditional funeral by reading an excerpt from a letter my son wrote to me while he was stationed overseas."

Ian reached into his pocket and pulled out the envelope containing Alexander's final letter. With trembling hands, he carefully unfolded the letter. Everyone waited anxiously to hear what words the letter contained. Ian cleared his parched throat, took a sip of water, and began reading...

Dear Dad,

If you are reading this letter, it means I am no longer alive. Thanks to you, however, I believe that death isn't the final destination in our long path of life. Thank you for raising me to be a good man and for guiding me with your always-strong faith. I have one request to make for my funeral. Christian and I taught the children's choir a special song. Please have them sing it for me as I lay before my friends and family.

Love, your son,
Alexander

Ian folded the letter and nodded to the youth choir director. Thirty children between the ages of four and ten walked up to the altar and formed a circle around Alexander's casket, holding hands as they faced him. The music played, and the children beautifully sang "Angels Among Us."

Everyone in the church joined them in singing. When the last notes echoed off the church walls, not one eye in the entire church remained dry. Even the stoic Colonel Andrews had to get a tissue from Isabelle.

Ian reflected upon the words of the song for a few minutes and then finished with the rest of the traditional funeral service. When Ian finished, he nodded to Colonel Andrews.

Six Red Bulls from Alexander's unit had accompanied Colonel Andrews to the church: their special assignment was to serve as Alexander's pallbearers. The Colonel gave the detail leader a signal, and the six Red Bulls went up to the casket, picked it up onto their shoulders, and carried it down the long aisle of the church, their steps slow and deliberate. Outside the front doors, in the frigid cold of the Minnesota weather, the Red Bulls slid Alexander's casket into the waiting hearse with care.

The long funeral procession of nearly one-hundred and fifty cars making the two-mile drive to the cemetery was a moving sight. Over two-thousand people braved the sub-zero wind chills to pay their final respects to Alexander. The residents of Columbus lined both sides of the street, waving American flags as the hearse carrying Alexander's body drove past them. Men, women, boys, and girls, both young and old, had come out to say goodbye to their fallen hero, disregarding the cold and the falling snow. Military veterans from all branches of the service braved the harsh elements too, donning their old uniforms with medals proudly displayed on their chests, to salute Alexander when the black hearse drove past them.

Waiting at the cemetery were an additional fifteen Red Bulls. Three buglers had positioned themselves about twenty-five yards from the gravesite. The four-member color guard stood near the gravesite, holding the American flag, the Army flag, and the flag of the Red Bulls. Seven riflemen and the detail leader took up a position sixty yards away on top of a small hill.

When all the friends and family members were in place around Alexander's grave, Colonel Andrews gave the nod to begin. The funeral director fought the stiff wind as he opened the back of the hearse, and the six Red Bull pallbearers slid Alexander's casket out. The moment Alexander's flag-draped casket came into view, Colonel Andrews and the fifteen Red Bulls snapped to attention and saluted their fallen comrade-in-arms. With slow and cautious steps, the pallbearers carried the casket over the slippery snow-covered ground to the gravesite and placed it onto the bier.

Colonel Andrews barked out "order arms," then "parade rest." The Red Bulls dropped their rigid salutes and stood at ease. Colonel Andrews nodded to Ian to proceed with the interment service.

The unfavorable weather worsened with each passing minute. The once-small, light snowflakes were growing in size and density, blanketing the ground in heavy, wet snow. The stinging bite of a freezing wind added to the unforgiving weather.

Ian raised his voice above the constant whistling of the northwest wind to say a few short words about his son, then led everyone in the Lord's Prayer. When he finished, Ian nodded to Colonel Andrews to proceed with the rendering of honors.

Colonel Andrews barked out "attention" as loud as he could so all the Red Bulls would hear him. They all snapped to attention. He bellowed out "present arms," and all the Red Bulls saluted their fallen brother. Next he signaled to the detail leader of the rifle squad, who acknowledged the Colonel's signal, then commanded, "ready, aim, and fire."

The seven riflemen's shots rang out, piercing the freezing afternoon air. Isabelle and Abigail flinched, startled by the earsplitting rifle blasts. Two more times, the riflemen fired volleys over Alexander's casket. The strident rifle barrage resonated loudly but was quickly swallowed up in the cold, howling wind.

The three bugle players stepped into position in a triangle, the lead bugler facing Alexander's casket and the other two facing away from the gravesite, to represent the American flag, soon to be folded into a triangle and presented to the next of kin. The lead bugler played "Silver

Echo Taps" flawlessly, while the other two buglers created a haunting echo effect.

As the last note faded away, the six pallbearers lifted the American flag from Alexander's casket and folded it into a tight triangle as the casket was lowered into the cold, frozen ground.

The detail assistant handed the flag to Colonel Andrews. He marched over to stand in front of Isabelle and, looking earnestly into her eyes, spoke the traditional military words of thanks for a fallen comrade: "This flag is presented on behalf of a grateful nation and the United States Army as a token of appreciation for your loved one's honorable and faithful service." With the final words, Colonel Andrews presented the folded American flag to Isabelle.

"Thank you," Isabelle murmured, her words barely audible even to the Colonel. Abigail hugged her mother, and their tears froze to their cheeks as they fell.

With the interment service officially over, Colonel Andrews presented a display case holding three shell casings, one from each rifle volley, to Isabelle and explained, "These three spent shell casings represent duty, honor, and country."

"Thank you again, Colonel," she said, her faint words drowned by the wind.

Arm in arm, Isabelle and Abigail walked through the wet snow to Abigail's car. After brushing the snow from the windshield, they began the slow drive home to prepare for the guests coming to celebrate Alexander's life.

Ian walked over to Colonel Andrews and shook his hand. "I'd like to thank you and your men for providing a beautiful burial for my son. If any of you care to join us at our home for the celebration of Alexander's life, you're more than welcome."

"Thank you, Mr. Havily. I'll stop by to celebrate your son's life and legacy," the Colonel said, then turned and trudged toward his vehicle.

Snowfall approaching three inches had covered the small town of Columbus in just ninety minutes. Ian looked up at the dark snow-filled clouds rolling through the turbulent sky, squinting as the large snowflakes stuck to his eyelashes. As he looked heavenward, he tried to find a way to believe, to recover the faith he had lost, but he saw only large, grey clouds callously dumping their contents on him and his son's grave. To Ian it felt as if God were brandishing a saltshaker filled with white poison over his head. His cheeks throbbed in pain as the merciless icy northwest winds stung his tender face like a thousand hornets.

"So, Lord, is that your final answer to me?" Ian muttered to himself. He tried in vain to understand the cruelty of it all. His heart was empty, a vacuum of nothingness. All seemed worthless, hopeless. Nowhere did Ian's soul find the presence of God. Bible in hand, he put his head down and plodded to his car, alone.

Upon reaching his vehicle, Ian looked back and squinted hard, trying to make out Alexander's final resting place, but all he could see was a hypnotic curtain of falling snow. Like the closing curtain on the final run of a short-lived Broadway show, it signaled the end of the once-promising and beautiful life of Alexander Havily, a life ended much too soon.

Ian dropped to his knees and loudly cursed the Lord, his words soon lost in the whistling of the freezing wind. The heavy snow collected on Ian's bowed head, matching the weight in his heart, until he gradually rose and slid into the driver's seat. He started the ignition, then put his head on the steering wheel and sobbed.

Chapter 21

MILES AWAY

Ian arrived home, shocked to see over one hundred cars in his driveway. He'd thought the adverse weather conditions would make most people skip the celebration of life for Alexander. He reached over for his bible and stepped out into the deep snow.

Ian put his head down as the strong, snow-filled wind chafed his face like the rough strokes of a cat's tongue. The sidewalk was easy to find, since dozens of footprints pressed down the fresh white powder on the ground. He walked up the porch steps and stopped at the door to brush off the snow as best he could and remove the bulk of what clung to his shoes. He stepped into his warm, inviting home. The snow covering the door's stained glass windows fell in a heap onto the porch as he shut the door behind him.

Ian removed his wet overcoat and shoes and put on his warm, fuzzy slippers. Bible in hand, he walked through the house, greeting and thanking his guests for braving the weather to celebrate Alexander's life. He found Abigail and Isabelle at the antique table with photo albums, showing off pictures of Alexander as a baby. He hugged Isabelle from behind but ignored his daughter with cold disdain.

Ian excused himself and walked into his private office. He locked the door behind him and set the bible on top of his desk. Chilled down to the bone, he decided to start a fire in the fireplace. It would be some time before the budding fire warmed the room's crisp air, and Ian wanted his inner core thawed, if only artificially and temporarily.

Ian sat down at his desk, opened a drawer, and removed a bottle of blackberry brandy and a crystal low-ball tumbler. He filled the tumbler to the brim and pounded down the brandy in one swift gulp. The liquor burned the entire way down, from his palate to his stomach, and his eyes watered violently, but Ian didn't care. He needed to feel something other than sorrow. He looked over at the bible Abigail had given him, resting on the edge of his desk. He picked it up and ran his fingers across its cover and binding. After a moment, he opened the bible and read aloud the loving inscription his daughter's young hand had written long ago: "Happy Birthday to the best dad in the whole wide world, love Abigail."

The anger and resentment that had been simmering inside Ian overtook his now-empty soul. He stood up and carried the bible over to the flames that danced hypnotically in the fireplace. Then he did the unimaginable: He threw his holy bible into the fire with a vindictive fury and stood in silence, watching it burn into ashes.

A loud knock on his office door awoke Ian from the flames' mesmerizing trance. He walked over to the door and unlocked it. Isabelle opened the door and looked curiously at her husband. He should be out visiting with their guests, she scolded. Ian apologized to his wife and followed her out of the sanctuary of his office.

Most people attending the celebration of Alexander's life stayed for only an hour or so due to the blizzard raging outside. Colonel Andrews was the last guest to leave. Ian shook the Colonel's hand with a firm grip and expressed his gratitude once again for the remarkable job the Red Bulls had done for his son. Isabelle and Abigail walked the Colonel to the door and gave him a warm hug before he stepped out into the snow-filled evening air.

Isabelle stopped in the kitchen to pour herself a glass of wine, and Abigail detoured to her bedroom to fetch the baby monitor. Then they both joined Ian at the dining room table.

The three sat in silence. The only sound that broke the stillness was soft cooing from the baby monitor. Abigail smiled, enthralled to hear the baby sounds coming from the monitor. Isabelle smiled, too, and squeezed Abigail's hand to offer comfort. Isabelle was an astute woman. She sensed Ian was blaming Abigail for Alexander's death, and she knew if she didn't intervene, his stubbornness could damage, maybe permanently ruin, the loving relationship he had always had with his daughter. Isabelle stood up, ready to confront Ian about his self-indulgence and misconception, when the phone rang.

Abigail rushed into the kitchen to answer it, praying Christian would be on the other end. She picked up the receiver. "Hello. This is the Havily household," she said. Her hands trembled, and her voice cracked.

"Abigail, it's me," Christian said softly.

Abigail's eyes closed in relief. "Where are you, my love?" She fought back the tears welling in her eyes.

In the dining room, Ian and Isabelle listened, absorbing every word Abigail spoke.

"I'm in the VA hospital in the Twin Cities," Christian explained. "I arrived about an hour ago. The doctors say I'll only be here overnight and they'll release me tomorrow morning."

"Oh, wonderful! I'll come pick you up first thing in the morning."

"No," Christian replied. "I'm not coming home. I'm dead inside. Dead to the world. Dead to you."

"Don't say that! Please. Don't ever say that again," Abigail pleaded desperately. She was losing her husband before he even returned home, and she didn't know what to say to him.

Christian's voice fell in sadness. "It's too late, Abigail. I can't fulfill anything I promised you. I'm not the man you need me to be. It's over for me... it's over for us."

When she heard the cruel click at the other end, Abigail fell to the floor, crying uncontrollably. He had hung up on her. He had quit on her.

Isabelle rushed to her daughter's side, and hugged her with a comfort only a mother could provide.

"He isn't coming home, Mom. He's never coming home!" Abigail sobbed. "He's at the VA hospital in the Twin Cities, just for tonight. He'll be released in the morning. He's going to disappear forever from me and his..."

Abigail fell silent the moment she heard the screams coming through the baby monitor. She ran up the stairs, Isabelle close on her heels, and rushed into the nursery. Abigail went over to the crib and picked up her frightened little one, cooing in a soft voice.

Isabelle stood in the doorway, proudly watching her beautiful daughter blossom as a loving parent. She walked over and rubbed her daughter's back as Abigail cradled the bundle of joy.

"Honey, let me hold the little one. I want you to go get your guitar and sing us a song," Isabelle said.

Abigail handed her mother the infant. Isabelle sat down in the rocking chair, her grandchild tucked in her arms. Abigail returned, guitar in hand. As she put the guitar strap over her shoulder, she looked over to her mother and child.

"Mom, why is Dad so angry with me? I never asked Alexander to sacrifice himself for Christian. I only asked for

Alexander to not tell Christian I was pregnant. Alexander promised me, on his own accord, he would watch over Christian and bring him home safely to me. Now Alexander is never coming home, and neither is Christian."

Isabelle looked at her daughter's despondent face and tried to calm her. "We'll drive over to the hospital first thing in the morning to pick up Christian, as soon as this blizzard passes by."

Over six inches of snow had fallen already, and the blizzard of the decade showed no signs of letting up. Abigail knew that by the time they arrived at the hospital the next day, it would be too late. Christian would be gone. If it weren't storming so hard, Abigail thought, I'd go get him right now.

"Play us something beautiful, Abigail, please," Isabelle said.

"I don't know what to play."

"Do what you do best, dear. Play what you feel deep inside," her mother urged.

Abigail strummed her guitar, trying to find an inner inspiration, but none would come to her sorrowful heart. But when she looked at the beautiful bundle of joy cradled in her mother's arms, her inner muse spoke.

The notes of "Miles Away" rolled off the guitar. As Abigail sang the heartfelt words of longing, it became clear she was singing to Christian. Every passionate word she sang echoed a profound love, but also a deep sadness in missing someone who wasn't home but should've been. Isabelle cried as her daughter sang the tender words.

Isabelle wasn't the only Havily crying. Abigail and Isabelle had forgotten they'd left the baby monitor on the dining room table. Ian had heard every word of the song. More important, he'd heard every solemn word of the conversation preceding the song.

Ian stared at the baby monitor in disbelief, his brain working to absorb what he had heard. Could it be true that

Abigail hadn't asked Alexander to watch over Christian? That Alexander was the one who offered to protect him? A small miracle occurred at the dining room table. The extinguished pilot light to Ian's cold heart began to flicker. Slowly but steadily, Ian's wounded heart warmed, and a great indelible love renewed his soul.

Ian slammed his fist down on the table at his stupidity, his selfish actions, and his unfair mistreatment of his beloved daughter. Suddenly, he jumped up and raced to the front closet. He kicked off his warm slippers and put on his shoes and overcoat. He dug around in the coat pockets, located his car keys, flung the door open, and ran out into the raging snowstorm, forgetting to even close the door behind himself.

He fell on his way to the car, but he jumped up and screamed out to the Lord that he wouldn't be stopped on his pilgrimage to bring Christian back home. A thick blanket of snow covered his car and ice sealed the doors, but Ian brushed and scraped his way in, falling into the driver's seat. The wind whistled like a siren as he fired up the engine and drove off into the blinding snow.

Upstairs in the nursery, Abigail and Isabelle heard the loud thump of Ian's fist on the table. They quickly put the one little one back into the crib and rushed downstairs. Isabelle found the front door standing open to the wrath of the blizzard and quickly shut it. When she went into the dining room, she found her daughter staring at the baby monitor on the table. Then it dawned on them: Ian had heard every word of their conversation.

"Mom, where did Dad go?" Abigail asked, apprehension in her voice.

Isabelle's eyes danced as she spoke. "If I know anything about your father, he went out into this terrible storm to get your husband and bring him home."

Chapter 22

QUANDARY

The time neared five in the evening. Christian stood alone by the frost-covered window in his hospital room. He wore a dark blue hospital gown that barely covered the way he was born into this world. The stubble on his face had grown prickly and coarse, like porcupine quills. Christian needed to shave but had no motivation to do so after the short telephone call with Abigail abruptly ended. She thought Christian had hung up on her, but the storm was the culprit that terminated the conversation.

The heavy winds had blown a tree into the power transformer that supplied the hospital with its energy, and although the emergency backup generator had kicked in, it could supply power to only the most vital operations. The backup lights, along with the fast-fading daylight seeping in through the windows, illuminated the room with an eerie faintness. Day and night blended into one, and the combination of the two forces cast a ghostly shadow upon the room.

Exhausted in every way imaginable, Christian's willpower was hemorrhaging away. His heart felt empty and shriveled, as though his lifeblood had been depleted, leaving only desiccated remains.

Christian stood in silence, staring out the window at the snowstorm. The mammoth snowflakes swirled as they fell from the sky, hypnotizing Christian into a deep trance, leaving him feeling lost to this world.

A loud knock at the door jolted him out of his dream world, and as fast as his injured body would allow, Christian slipped back into bed.

"Come in," he called.

The door swung open with an eerie silence. In walked someone who would be the roadblock to his escape from the hospital. She shut the door and took a few steps in.

A woman in her late twenties smiled at him. She wore a silver oak leaf insignia on the collar of her army uniform. Her light brown hair was tightly plaited and tied up in a stylish bun on the back of her head. Her body was slender and she appeared to have a fair complexion, but in the room's dim illumination, Christian couldn't tell the color of her eyes.

She introduced herself cordially while thumbing through Christian's personnel file. "My name is Major Syborn and I'm the resident psychiatrist here at the hospital. It's a pleasure to make your acquaintance."

"I don't need a shrink," he replied tersely, his voice cold.

"Well, I'm sorry to say you do need me, Specialist Bryson, unless, of course, you don't want to receive a discharge from the hospital tomorrow, or any day after that. I'm your one-way ticket out of here. Besides, if you say no, I'll have you tossed into the brig for insubordination. So, do you want to do this the easy way, or shall we do it the hard way? The choice is up to you."

This unforeseen predicament threw a big monkey wrench in Christian's plan to leave the hospital. He could see he held a losing hand and nodded to the leather chair next to his bed.

Major Syborn sat down. "I'm glad you're seeing things my way."

Christian rolled his eyes. "You remind me of my mother-in-law."

"You'd better watch your tongue, Specialist Bryson. This silver oak leaf I wear on my collar warrants your complete respect!"

"I'm sorry, ma'am. I'm just a little off kilter. I said some very harsh words to my wife on the telephone, and then the line went dead. I wish I could call her back, but I can't."

"Apology accepted," she said, her voice much softer than before. "Look, this session is just a formality. But it must be conducted, so let's try to make this as friendly as possible. You can call me by my first name, and I'll call you by yours."

"Isn't that against Army protocol, ma'am?"

She flashed him a smile. "Not if we keep it to ourselves."

"Okay ma'am. What's your first name?"

"Betsy," she replied with a wink.

"Okay then, Betsy... what is it you want to know?"

"Well, let me get the routine psychiatric question out of the way first. Tell me about your relationship with your mother."

Christian burst into laughter. He thought her question was irrelevant, but he was enormously mistaken.

"What's so funny?" she demanded, perturbed by his reaction to her serious question.

"Nothing at all," Christian said, "but I never knew my mother, never talked to her, never touched her, never saw her. She died within an hour of giving birth to me."

"I'm sorry, Christian. That is very heartrending indeed."

As they talked, Christian's frozen heart began to melt like an ice cube left out on the counter. He felt comfortable, safe even, talking with Betsy. "I think of my life as a kaleidoscope that is always changing, melding the colors of my life," he explained. "One minute you see something joyous, the next minute you see something tragic. My life right now resembles a dark quagmire shadowed in tragedy."

To his surprise, opening up made him feel a little better. He sat up in his bed, more attentive now. "So, what else do you want to know?"

"Well, I was going to ask about your father, but only if you promise not to laugh," she teased.

Christian didn't laugh. Instead, he closed his eyes and called up the wonderful memories of his father. "My dad was a great man. He sacrificed everything for me so I could lead a fulfilling life."

"Was a great man? Is he dead?" she asked, her voice courteous and gentle. She took care with her tone to not threaten or offend Christian, afraid he would close up like an oyster and hide his pearls of emotion.

Christian took a deep breath. "Yes, my father is dead. He died last year of bone cancer. Not a single day goes by that I don't miss him with all my heart."

"I'm positive he knows just how you feel about him."

"Thank you." Christian tried his best to put on a courageous face for Betsy, but he couldn't hide the deep sorrow in his soul. The pain in his heart seemed to exude from his tired, bloodshot eyes.

Betsy's heart went out to Christian as he struggled with his emotions. She had been writing in his dossier as he spoke, and now she looked up from its pages. "It says here you were pretty distraught when you learned about Specialist Havily's death."

"Please don't call him Specialist Havily. His name was Alexander!"

"Okay, Christian. Please tell me about Alexander."

"He was my best friend. He would've done anything for me, and apparently, he did. He sacrificed his life for mine. I should be the one buried six feet under the ground, not him. I haven't slept much since I learned he died," Christian explained. "Compound that with my medical condition and you can see why I have nightmares. I wake up shaking all over, in a cold sweat. I get an hour or two of sleep and then wake up, more exhausted than ever. Every day I get more and more weary and debilitated, yet I lie awake for most of night, haunted."

"Do you blame yourself for Alexander's death?"

Christian tightened his lips and contemplated long and hard. Finally, he answered. "It is what it is. That's the best answer I can come up with. Alexander and I were just doing our jobs in a dangerous situation. I don't remember any of it. All the information I have has come through my wife."

"Let's talk about your wife for a while, shall we?" Betsy sensed this would be another sensitive subject for Christian, and she was correct. His body language betrayed his guilt as he squirmed in his hospital bed. His mistreatment of Abigail was the one subject he didn't want to discuss with Betsy. Christian felt ashamed of his selfish words to the love of his life, and he thought he didn't deserve Abigail's love and loyalty. He had forsaken her when she needed him, and his immature actions haunted him, making both his stomach and his heart twist in pain.

"What would you like to know about Abigail?" Christian asked, his voice tentative.

"Just speak about anything that comes to your mind," Betsy replied, softly. Understanding and compassion were evident in her tone.

"Okay. I've known Abigail my entire life. We're alike in many ways. She's my mirror image, my soul mate, my best friend. Abigail has always been there for me, through thick and thin, during the good times and the bad. I've been a jerk to her, and pushed her away because of my insecurities. I need to get home to her, I need to apologize. None of this is her fault, but I don't know if she can ever accept the man I've become."

"It seems to me that you're on the correct path to redemption," Betsy said. "She's your wife and you're her husband. What makes you think she won't accept you or your apologies? After all, you're the love of each other's lives."

Christian paused. He recalled his dad's aversion to the cane that he thought stigmatized him as a broken man in the eyes of others. "I'm a cripple now, just like my father."

"Why do you feel that way?"

"I promised Abigail a family. We wanted to raise children together. Now, thanks to the shrapnel wound, I can't father any children. No surgery can fix the damage, and no counseling can mend the heartbreak over promises I can't keep. My promises are lost forever, just like my innocent belief that I could give my wife what she wanted. The worst thing, though, is looking at myself in the mirror. I see a man who is a fraud. That's why I pushed Abigail away, because I didn't want to face her. I don't know if I can ever look her in the eyes again, or promise her anything. The promises I made her are now nothing but hollow words."

Betsy stood up and walked over to the window. She gazed out at the raging blizzard, thinking about what Christian had said. "Christian, you must return to Abigail." She turned and looked him dead in the eyes. "Life is but a breath in time. Each second you spend hiding in fear is a wasted second you'll never get back. It's really as simple as that."

Christian's eyes welled up. Betsy was right. It was time to go home to Abigail.

"Will you release me tomorrow so I can go home?" he asked, hoping she'd say yes.

But Betsy didn't reply. She turned back to the wintry scene outside, and her eyes focused on the hypnotizing snow blowing in hard with the westerly wind. The furiously falling sheet of white signaled the arrival of the visitor she'd been expecting for quite some time. She turned to face

Christian, gazing on him with understanding compassion, and smiled.

Christian repeated his question.

This time, Betsy replied. "I promise everything will work out just fine for you. Trust me." Her voice echoed with confidence. "Now I must leave you. It was a pleasure to finally meet you." Betsy smiled and extended her hand to him.

"Finally?" he questioned, extending his own hand to shake hers.

Christian's question went unanswered. The moment their hands clasped, Christian's eyes rolled back and his eyelashes fluttered rapidly. He shook violently as if he were a convicted felon, strapped into the electric chair, paying for his transgressions with a flip of the executioner's switch. Betsy released her grasp and gazed at Christian, now in a deep slumber, dreaming, peaceful. Betsy supplanted his bad dreams with loving memories of his life, and for the first time in many days, Christian slept with no nightmares.

Betsy turned her attention back to the window. She looked outside and lost herself in the striking ambience of God's beautiful snowy-white masterpiece. Then, she closed her eyes and waited for her one true purpose: Ian.

Chapter 23

PROVIDENTIAL EDIFICATION

The intensity of the storm was much worse than any Ian had witnessed in his long life. But Ian was determined, and nothing, not even God himself, was going to stop him from his mission of bringing Christian home to his family. Ian was like the monomaniacal Captain Ahab, unwilling to concede to his ferocious white nemesis.

Ian's cell phone rang. Abigail was on the other end.

"Dad, where are you going?" she asked, nervous and apprehensive.

"I'm on my way to get your husband."

"I don't want you out in this weather. Please come home. It's not safe for you to drive in this blizzard."

"I promise if the conditions get too bad, I'll turn around. I can always try to get Christian again tomorrow."

The road was already horrendous, icy and as dangerous as Ian had ever seen. He'd lied to his daughter to settle her worries. He wouldn't be turning around no matter how bad the blizzard raged. He was going to get Christian, and now, not in the morning.

"I love you, Dad."

"I love you, too."

But she didn't hear his response. The storm's interference was too great.

"Dad... Dad... hello?" There was no reply. Her dad's cell phone had lost its signal.

Not another soul had ventured out into the night. Ian crept along, alone on the slippery road, top speed falling short of fifteen miles per hour. His goal was to make it to the hospital in one piece. His biggest fear: sliding off the icy road and into a snow-filled ditch. He'd have zero chance of rescue; his cell phone had no signal. Not that any rescuers would be able to find him anyway. The mounds of snow blew and rolled like sand dunes in the Sahara.

The thirty-five minute drive to the VA hospital took more than two hours, but motivated by his single-minded determination to reach Christian, Ian finally pulled his frosted, snow-covered car into the hospital parking lot around half past eight. The visitors' parking lot was devoid of life, engulfed in darkness, and covered almost knee deep in heavy, wet snow. Ian parked where the snow seemed the shallowest and peered out of his windshield. He couldn't believe he had made it. During the worst of the drive, he thought that God was punishing him for cursing His name and desecrating the holy bible.

Ian stepped out of his vehicle into the snow and merciless wind that whipped around his body. He turned straight into the tempest and held his head high, almost as if he were begging for the snow to blast away his contemptuous transgressions against God.

Ian made his way across the dark parking lot to the hospital's entrance and fought the furious wind to pry open the door. He burst into the inviting warmth of the hospital's vestibule, then stomped his feet and brushed the snow off his clothes onto the entrance mat.

Ian looked around the empty vestibule, then entered the silent reception area. No signs of life, anywhere. Only rolling tumbleweeds were needed to complete the hospital's impression of a ghost town. The dim lighting provided by the emergency generator added to the peculiar atmosphere.

The uncanny silence was broken by the loud, sudden cough of the night watchman seated at the security desk. The sound rippled through the hushed stillness like a rock heaved into a lake. Ian walked over to the security desk and noticed that the guard, a Corporal in the military police, was reading the bible.

"Excuse me, Corporal. I'm here for Specialist Bryson."

The Corporal looked up, irritated by the disturbance. "I'm sorry, sir. It's after visiting hours. I can't let you in." He returned to his bible.

Ian thought quickly, then unbuttoned his overcoat and pointed to his cassock and the small, white square in the front of his collar. "Official church business," Ian lied. "This is an emergency. I didn't drive for more than two hours in this hellacious storm so you could turn me away from administering last rights to a dying soldier because it's after visiting hours. Do you want that on your conscience, Corporal?" Ian glared at the Corporal with menacing eyes.

"No, sir. Sorry, sir." The Corporal's demeanor had made an about face. Cooperative and apologetic now, he handed Ian a visitor's name badge and instructed him to clip it onto his overcoat.

"Thank you," Ian said. "What's his room number and how do I get to him?"

"Room 213, sir. Go down the hall and take the first left. After about twenty feet, you'll come to elevators. Take one up to the second floor."

"Thank you again, Corporal."

Ian followed the Corporal's directions, and in a few minutes he stood at the closed door of room 213. He took a deep breath and looked up, asking the Lord for some spiritual guidance. Ian didn't know that on the other side of the door was a butterfly from heaven with a divine purpose. That wonderful butterfly was his old and very dear friend.

Ian opened the door and slipped into Christian's room. The lighting was darker than it had been in the hallway, and Ian's eyes took a moment to adjust to the dimness. As they did, he spotted the silhouette of a woman standing at the window, her back toward him. He took a step forward, cautious in his attempt to get a better look at her. Christian appeared sound asleep, but it was hard to tell in the darkness.

Ian squinted. "Excuse me, miss. What are you doing in my son-in-law's room?" He didn't want to provoke this unknown person in the shadows.

"I'm spending a bit of time with my son, if you don't mind," she replied softly.

Ian recognized the voice, but he couldn't believe what he was hearing. The woman turned around and stepped into the faint light. Ian's eyes widened in disbelief and his heart skipped a beat, then another, as Elizabeth's young face emerged from the shadows. She had not aged a single day in twenty-one years.

"Hello, Ian. I told you I'd see you again one day."

Ian's hands trembled and his knees knocked. He had no idea what to do or say.

"Don't be afraid. I've been waiting for this day, waiting for you." Elizabeth's comforting smile radiated warmth in the faint light.

"Why are you waiting for me?" Ian asked. "I don't understand. Aren't you here to see Christian?"

"No, Ian. I'm here to see you."

"But Christian needs your help more than I do."

"You're mistaken. Christian knows what he wants. He was just too afraid to go get it. But you, Ian, are drifting, aimless, without a purpose. It's time to mend the tear in your heart."

Ian caught a glimpse of the nametag attached to her uniform. "Syborn? Does Christian know that you're his mother?"

"No. And he won't for now. He needs to focus on himself and his family."

Elizabeth pointed to the chair beside the bed and instructed him to take a seat. "Buckle up. We're going for the ride of your life."

Ian couldn't take his eyes off Elizabeth, despite his nervousness in her presence.

"My purpose was given to me a long time ago, Ian. My purpose is to save your lost soul."

"What are you going to do?"

Elizabeth walked behind Ian's chair, leaned forward, and whispered one word into his attentive ear: "edification." She placed her hands on his head and his eyelashes started to flutter. He fought the divine current flowing through his body and went rigid. The room went black, enveloping him in a shroud of darkness.

The darkness faded, replaced by a soft white light, and Ian found himself standing in his dining room. Before him, Abigail and Christian sat at the table, unmoving. They appeared frozen in time. Elizabeth stood next to Ian, dressed in a white robe with a white sash. To Ian's eyes, everything was shaded in black and white, except for a piece of jewelry in Elizabeth's flowing hair. The iridescent black and orange Monarch butterfly barrette was the only splash of color in the room.

"What does this mean, Elizabeth? How come we're in my dining room?"

"We're in the whispers of your family's yesterdays. Your son and Christian found out about their deployment this day, and your daughter learned of her pregnancy."

"Why is everything in black and white?"

"Only through God can you see the colors of the past," she whispered with reverence.

"Why did you bring me here?"

"So you can see the truth of what happened this day." With a wave of her hand, life returned to the dining room.

Ian and Elizabeth watched as Christian left for his dad's house and Alexander confronted his sister about lying to Christian. Ian listened intently as Abigail made her brother promise to keep her pregnancy a secret, nothing more. Ian cried when he heard Alexander freely offer his sister a promise: *"I'll watch out for Christian every day and protect him. I'll make sure he comes home alive and safe to you and your baby. This, Abigail, I promise you."*

Elizabeth waved her hand. The room froze, then faded from sight. She looked at Ian, and shook her head. "You've been punishing your daughter for something she didn't do."

Ian, overcome with guilt and shame for his treatment of Abigail, didn't reply.

Again, Elizabeth waved her hand, and the checkpoint and roadblock, frozen in black and white, came into view. Before them was Christian, standing guard. "This is the day Christian died," Elizabeth explained.

"Don't you mean Alexander?"

"No. I mean Christian."

Her words mystified him. Alexander was the one who had died. But before he could ask again, Elizabeth waved her hand and the scene came alive.

They watched as explosions sent shrapnel into Christian. His dead body dropped to the ground like a marionette whose strings had been cut. Elizabeth waved her hand, and again, the scene froze. She and Ian stood over Christian's lifeless body.

"As I told you, Christian died this day," she said softly.

"I don't understand... How could he come home alive?"

"Only God can answer your question. All I can do is show you the truth as to what happened here this day."

Elizabeth waved her hand again, and the scene before them showed Alexander under fire. Ian watched with difficulty as the morbid scene unfolded: the sniper bullet tearing into Alexander's shoulder, his determined crawl to reach Christian, and his struggle to throw himself over

Christian's lifeless body. Ian listened with a heavy heart to the words Alexander spoke to Christian as he lay over him, protecting him. Then, Ian witnessed the horror of the second sniper bullet tearing into Alexander's neck, the bullet that severed the chain his son wore and stole his life away.

Elizabeth waved her hand and froze the gruesome scene. Ian turned away, unable to look at his son's mangled body. He didn't see Elizabeth kneel down beside Alexander and Christian's bodies, pick up the silver cross, and slip it into the pocket of her white robe. She waved her hand and the scene faded away.

"The images are gone, Ian." Elizabeth put her soft hand on his shoulder, and the horror and grief that had overcome him disappeared.

Ian dried his eyes with the sleeve of his black cassock. When he looked up, he and Elizabeth stood in a small, white room. The room had no doors or windows, no furniture or decorations, nothing to interrupt the white emptiness.

"What is this place?" he asked.

"This is your purgatory. The path you're now following in life is leading you to this room. Unless you can change and find faith again, this is your destiny. I've provided you with some answers that have helped heal your heart. But filling it with love and faith again is up to you." Elizabeth smiled, and the vibrant green of her eyes reappeared. They sparkled and shimmered like brilliant emeralds.

"Elizabeth, are you an angel?"

"That question has a complicated answer. I like to think of living people as caterpillars and death a temporary cocoon until the spirit is released as a beautiful butterfly."

Ian gazed at the resplendent Monarch butterfly barrette resting in her flowing brown hair, and realization struck him.

"The Monarch butterfly that alighted on the church skylight the day I married Christian and Abigail... that was you, wasn't it?"

Elizabeth didn't answer his question. She looked into his eyes with profound happiness. "Ian, it's time for you to travel down your path in life. I've shown you the fork in the road. Now it's up to you to decide which path you will follow."

Sadness clung to Ian's voice. "Will I ever see you again?"

Elizabeth smiled. "I don't know, but I have this strange feeling we will meet again."

Elizabeth opened her arms to Ian and he gave his dear old friend a hug. The moment they embraced, he started to shake. Energy coursed through his body, but this time, he didn't fight the current. He gave himself up to the divine force flowing through him.

Chapter 24

THAT LONG ROAD HOME

Christian and Ian awoke at the same time from their deep and peaceful dreams. The storm of the decade was tapering off, and the early morning sun peeked warily through the dissipating clouds. Christian laughed upon finding his father-in-law sitting in the chair next to his hospital bed. The two of them looked at each other and rubbed the sleep from their weary eyes.

With one brow raised, Ian eyed his son-in-law. "You look like hell." Ian grimaced when he sat up and stretched out the kinks he'd gotten from sleeping in a chair.

"As do you." Christian sat up in bed and peered out the window at the white sea of snow.

"How are you feeling, son?"

"Terrible."

"How bad are your injuries?" Ian asked.

"That's not what I meant. I feel terrible about the way I've treated Abigail. She deserves better than that."

"You're not the only one in that boat. I've treated her horribly, too. What do you say we break out of here and go home to her?"

Concern clouded Christian's face. "Do you think she'll ever find it in her heart to forgive me?"

"I'm pretty sure she'll forgive us both. She has a forgiving heart. Let's give her a call." Ian pulled his cell phone from his pocket. There was still no signal. "Try the phone by your bed."

Christian stretched for the phone on the small bedside table. He shook his head. "This line is dead, too."

"Why don't you go ahead and get cleaned up. I'll try to find a doctor and see if we can get you released."

Christian nodded to his father-in-law and walked into the bathroom. To his surprise, his army dress uniform lay on the counter, neatly pressed and folded. He didn't know how it had gotten there, but he was happy to have some clothes to wear. He stepped into the shower with his razor and shaving cream. The hot water hitting his injuries stung at first. Then his wounded, scabbed-over body relaxed and he soaked in the moisture and warmth. Thirty minutes later, a shaved, showered, dressed, and refreshed Christian stepped out of the bathroom.

Ian greeted him with a smile, then handed him his release paperwork. "It looks like everything's in order and we can leave whenever you want."

Christian folded the paperwork and stuffed it into his pants pocket.

* * *

Christian waited in the warmth of the hospital's vestibule while Ian scraped off and warmed up the car, then maneuvered it around and through the deep drifts of snow to the entrance. For Ian, the drive went much faster than it had the night before. He was happy to see his tax dollars hard at work in the form of snowplows salting and sanding the roads, moving wave after wave of deep snow into the ditch. The two men said little on the trip home.

About two miles from home, Ian's cell phone rang, breaking the silence.

"Dad, where are you?" Abigail asked.

Ian could tell with certainty from the crack in her voice that his daughter was worried and nervous. "Christian and I are about two miles away."

"You have Christian with you?" Had she heard her father correctly? Her heart raced, wild with excitement. The anticipation of seeing Christian put butterflies in her tummy.

"Yes. He's with me, and we're almost home. We'll see you in a few minutes."

Ian ended the phone call with his delighted daughter and glanced over at Christian. His son-in-law looked nervous, and his hands fidgeted. When Ian pulled into his long, snow-covered driveway, Christian finally spoke.

"I never told you about my injuries. Most were superficial, but one was anything but. A piece of shrapnel ended my ability to father children. That's why I didn't want to come home to Abigail. I promised her a family, but I can't give her children. I know Abigail will be heartbroken when I tell her."

Ian burst into laughter, understanding now the reason for Christian's uncharacteristic actions.

"What's so damn funny about what I just said?" Christian glared at his father-in-law, his face red with anger. He failed to find any humor in his tragic plight.

"I'm not laughing at your injuries. I'm laughing about God's mysterious ways. Abigail will love you no matter what happens. Always remember that."

Ian parked his car, and he and Christian stepped out into the deep snow. Abigail and Isabelle waited on the porch in their large, puffy jackets, impatient to welcome their husbands home. As Christian walked toward the house, tears streamed down his cheeks. Abigail rushed down the porch steps to the love of her life, crying harder with each difficult step she took through the knee-deep snow. They met in a fervent embrace, absorbing each other's love for the first time in over nine months. Arm in arm, Ian and Isabelle watched their daughter and son-in-law's hearts find one another again.

Abigail loosened her embrace. She wanted to kiss her true love, but Christian fell to his knees in the snow and buried his head in her puffy jacket. He didn't have the strength to look into her eyes. Abigail put her hands on his tear-covered cheeks and tried to get him to look at her.

"Christian, what's wrong? Why won't you look at me?"

"I'm so sorry for everything I put you through, for everything you had to endure," Christian cried in disgrace. He kept his head buried in her jacket, hiding his shame from her.

"Everything will be okay. I promise." Abigail tenderly ran her fingers through his hair, trying to ease the fear she sensed in him but didn't understand.

Christian cringed inside when he heard the words "I promise." He mustered up all his strength and looked into her teary eyes. "Abigail, I made some promises to you I can now never fulfill," he said through heartbreaking sobs.

"What on earth are you talking about, my love?"

"I promised you a family, but… I've received a shrapnel injury that…" he paused, still searching for the words. "I can't father a child for you. I'm so sorry. I can't keep my promise. I can't fulfill your desire to be a mother."

Christian buried his head in her jacket again. He hadn't even noticed the weight gain in her face caused by her pregnancy.

"Christian, stand up. There's something I need to show you." Abigail took Christian's hands, pulled him up from his knees, and led him through the snow and into the house. Ian and Isabelle followed them inside.

"I have some unfinished business with you, too, when you're ready," Ian said. "Isabelle and I will be waiting for you at the dining room table."

Abigail smiled at her father, but Christian's weary mind still lingered on the disappointment he thought he'd brought home. Abigail squeezed his hand and led him up the stairs to the spare bedroom. She stopped at the closed door of the room, now converted into a nursery, and smiled reassuringly at Christian.

"What are we doing here?" a puzzled Christian asked, wiping his tear-stained face.

"You did keep your promise, my love. Every word of what you promised has come true. We're parents!" Abigail's light blue eyes filled with tears of joy at finally being able to tell him the secret she had kept for so long.

A look of disbelief washed over Christian's face. He couldn't believe his ears, couldn't process it all. He stood frozen in front of the door like a block of ice.

"Open the door and see the fulfillment of your promise to me," Abigail whispered. She understood what a shock this was for him and rubbed his back, thawing his apprehension with her gentle touch.

With a trembling hand, he slowly pushed the door open. He took one step into the nursery and gasped in astonishment at what he saw.

Abigail's soft touch soothed and healed Christian, dissipating the turmoil buried in his soul. "I love you so much," she said, her arm warmly encircling his waist. For the first time since Alexander died, Christian believed he and Abigail would have a miraculous life together.

Abigail led Christian to the crib on the right, and they looked down to the beautiful baby boy sleeping in his blue pajamas. "This is your son, Christian. His name is Alexander Noah Bryson. He'll carry on the legacy of your family name. I named him after my brother and your father because both men were great influences in our lives."

Christian's heart filled with awe and pride. He smiled down at his son and understood what his father must have felt so long ago when he became a dad.

Abigail then led Christian to the crib on the left, and they looked down to see a beautiful baby girl. Christian's heart filled with joy. "This is your daughter, Eilir Elizabeth Bryson," Abigail said. "She will forever be your darling little angel. I named her after the beautiful Monarch butterfly we saw at the cemetery and after your mother."

Christian was at a loss for words, save one: "Twins," he whispered. Christian watched his son and daughter sleep, dreaming of the pleasant lives they were going to live. Abigail stood behind Christian and hugged him tight.

Christian turned to his wife, who was still wearing her puffy jacket. He unzipped it, took it off her, and threw it on the rocking chair, then took her in his arms, kissing and caressing her with great appreciation and admiration. Abigail's body tingled from her pretty little toes up through her spine and into her head. She rubbed Christian's neck and back while his tender lips and soft hands worked their magic on her. Then she kissed him in the exact same way he had kissed her when he deployed months earlier. Right there, at that very moment in time, standing in the nursery with the sleeping babies they created together, Abigail and Christian's longing hearts found each other once again and beat blissfully in true harmony.

After some time, Christian began to think about it all and had some questions. "When did we conceive our children?"

"The night of our honeymoon, on the tugboat, the night that we made love for the first time. I have something to tell you: The day you told me about your deployment is the day I found out I was pregnant."

"Why didn't you tell me you were pregnant?"

"Because... the night of our honeymoon, on the tugboat. You lost it and my greatest fear was having your mind not on your duty. I needed you to come home alive, and so did our children."

Christian nodded. He understood. But then another difficult question popped into Christian's head and he needed to know the answer. "Did Alexander know you were pregnant before we deployed?"

Abigail looked deep into her husband's eyes. "Yes," she answered softly.

Christian closed his eyes and sighed. Everything that had been torturing his mind, his heart, and his soul had become clear with that one word. Now he understood why Alexander sacrificed his life. It was to make sure he returned home to Abigail and his progeny. Alexander had given Christian a second chance at life.

"I need you to go with me to the cemetery. To show me where Alexander is buried." Christian said. "I need to talk to him."

"Let's go downstairs and check in with my mom and dad first. We need to ask them to watch our children before I can drive you to the cemetery."

Christian nodded and took Abigail's hand. Together they walked out of the peaceful and hushed sanctum of their babies' nursery.

Chapter 25

A MOTHER'S GIFT

Christian and Abigail walked, hand in hand, down the staircase and into the dining room. Seated at the antique table, awaiting their company, were Ian and Isabelle. A medium-size box, wrapped in bright red wrapping paper and a gold bow, rested in the middle of the table.

"Christian, Abigail, I have something to talk to you both about. Please sit down with us," Ian said, his voice tender and warm.

Christian and Abigail walked over, sat down next to one another across from Ian, and waited for him to speak.

Ian looked at his wife, who gave him a subtle head nod. He then focused his attention onto his daughter, gazing at her with guilty eyes.

"What is it, Dad?"

"I owe you a huge apology, Abigail. Much to my shame, I blamed you indirectly for Alexander's death. I was wrong and I'm sorry. Please, I beg you to forgive me."

Abigail went over to her dad and put her arms around him. Ian held her in a long, heartfelt embrace, and Abigail cherished feeling her father's warm love once again.

"I forgive you, Daddy. I love you so much."

Ian smiled and, swallowing back his tears, tenderly kissed his daughter's forehead.

Ian next turned to his son-in-law. "Christian, the gift before you is from your mother. She charged me with its safekeeping on the day you were born, just minutes before she died. Her explicit instructions were to make sure you received it when you became a father yourself. It's been locked in my office safe for the better part of twenty-one years. Now, I fulfill my promise to your mother and present this gift to you."

Speechless, Christian sat motionless in his chair, staring at the box until Abigail nudged him in the ribs, breaking his engrossed gaze. Christian pulled the gift to himself and with trembling hands tore off the red wrapping paper. Underneath was a brown cardboard box, sealed with packing tape. Christian peeled off the tape and opened the box to find a sea of packing peanuts. His shaky hands waded among them, looking for his sunken treasure.

His hands locked onto something hard, and he looked at Ian, Isabelle, and Abigail, excitement flooding his eyes. Everyone leaned in closer to get a better look at what Christian had pulled out, and their eyes widened in amazement. A beautiful, ornate jewelry box, about eighteen inches long and twelve inches high and deep, now rested on the table. It was crafted from what looked like dark, petrified wood. Elegantly hand painted on the lid was an orange and black Monarch butterfly with white spots around the edges of its wings. On the front was a gold flap, protecting the key hole. Christian tried to open the jewelry box, but it was locked.

Christian and Abigail locked eyes. "The butterfly key!" they exclaimed at the same time.

"I'll get it!" Abigail flew upstairs to the nightstand next to her bed. She retrieved the key and sprinted back downstairs to hand it to Christian.

Christian moved the gold flap, inserted the highly wrought butterfly key, and turned it counterclockwise until he heard a pronounced click. It had unlocked the jewelry box with ease.

The anticipation in the dining room had been mounting slowly and steadily, and that *"click"* was like the climax in a thrilling suspense novel. Soon, the precious and mysterious treasure, locked away for years, would be revealed!

Christian opened the hinged lid carefully and cautiously. Inside, he found a note folded in half, written on pristine white paper that, amazingly, hadn't yellowed through the years. Underneath he found four presents wrapped in different colors of wrapping paper. Christian unfolded the letter and read aloud…

My Dearest Christian,

If you are reading this letter, my son, then you must now know you are the father of twins, a boy and a girl. If I were to venture a guess, I would say you're sitting at the antique dining room table with Ian and Isabelle and your wife Abigail.

Christian stopped reading for a moment. He looked to his wife and in-laws, who were as shocked as he was. How did his mother know he was the father of twins, or that Abigail was his wife's name? Abigail wasn't even born yet when his mother died. Incredulous, he looked back down to the letter and started to read aloud again…

There are four gifts inside this jewelry box, one for each of you seated at the table. Each is a little miracle that will reinforce your deep belief in God. Christian, your present is in the blue wrapping paper. Abigail's is orange, Ian's is green, and Isabelle's is silver. Always remember to honor and cherish one another's love as well as God's love. All my purposes are complete, and now I can rest in eternal peace next to my beloved husband.

I love you all very much,
Elizabeth

Christian folded the note, laid it back in the jewelry box, and handed each person the correct present from Elizabeth. All four of them were numb, shocked by the revelations in the note. This was not accidental. What they were experiencing was something different. This was a plan from God, and they were all part of it.

Christian smiled through the tears beginning to form in his eyes. "Abigail, please open your gift first."

All eyes focused on Abigail as she tore into the orange wrapping. Under the paper was a small red box, much like the one her engagement ring was in the day Christian proposed. Abigail opened the red box, and to her astonishment, a beautiful crystal Monarch butterfly barrette, vividly colored orange and black with white spots on its wings, rested inside. She removed the resplendent piece of jewelry with care and fastened it to her soft brown hair. Ian recognized the barrette the moment he saw it. Elizabeth was wearing it when he saw her during the flashbacks at the hospital.

"You're next, Mom," Christian said.

Isabelle removed the silver wrapping paper from her gift and found a box like Abigail's, except it was a little smaller and white. When she opened it, Isabelle's eyes fell on the treasure inside: the silver cross she had bestowed on Alexander before he deployed. Isabelle picked up the cross, turned it over, and stared in disbelief. To her delight and surprise, engraved on the back side was Alexander's name. Alexander's cross had come home to her.

Christian looked to Ian and nodded. Ian's gift was larger than the others. He ripped off the green wrapping paper and, to his astonishment, held in his hands the bible Abigail had given him long ago. He opened the cover and reread the inscription she had written in her childish hand. He had his precious bible back from the ashes, and also his daughter's forgiveness. Ian's once-empty heart filled with love and faith again.

"Why was the bible I gave you when I was a little girl in the jewelry box?" Abigail asked.

"It's a long story that we can discuss later. Let's just say the bible was there for a reason." Ian smiled at his daughter as he held his favorite gift from her.

All eyes now turned to Christian, who held his unopened present in his hands. Christian looked to them all and smiled. Then, he removed the blue wrapping paper. The present: a photo album. When he opened it, his eyes filled with awe and disbelief. In every picture—Major Syborn. The woman in the hospital, whom he had shared so much with, was his mother.

Christian dug the hospital discharge paperwork out of his pants pocket and looked at the signature on the release form. Syborn. Realization then dawned on him. He needed to unscramble the letters. "Syborn... Syborn... Syborn..." he muttered under his breath. Christian worked as fast as he could to rearrange the letters. Then, he saw it: *Bryson.* After all these years, Christian had photos of his mother to cherish. For that, he was grateful to God.

"I need to call the hospital," Christian said, standing up.

Ian grabbed his arm and stopped him dead in his tracks. "Christian, you won't find what you're looking for at the hospital. I already called, when you were upstairs with Abigail. No one has ever heard of a Major Syborn. But I met her while you were sleeping, and I know who she was. I never left the room while you showered and dressed. I fell asleep, and your discharge paperwork was inside my cassock pocket when I awoke."

Christian understood what Ian was trying to tell him and returned to his seat. For a long while he, Abigail, Ian, and Isabelle sat in silence at the antique dining room table, thinking about the Lord's miracle they had all been a part of.

Abigail turned to her parents. "Christian would like me to drive him to the cemetery so he can visit Alexander's grave."

Ian shook his head. "The headstones are buried under the snow. You'll have a trying time locating his gravesite. The temperature is supposed to return to the mid-fifties in the next few days. Maybe it's best to give the sun a few days to melt the snow away. Christian, spend some time with your son and daughter and heal up a little more. Then Isabelle and I will drive you both to the cemetery."

Christian agreed, with reluctance, to his father-in-law's suggestion. He spent the next three days bonding with Alexander Noah and Eilir Elizabeth. And each night, he held Abigail in his arms. He kissed her neck and rubbed her tummy with affection, and traced the words "I love you" on the soft skin of her back.

On the fourth day, Ian drove the entire family, including the newborns, to the cemetery. Christian asked for a moment alone at his parents' graves first. He trudged through the snow, now only about a foot deep, to his parents' graves, where he brushed the snow off the headstone and the old wooden bench. He sat down and started to speak right away. He'd had three days to think of what he wanted to tell his parents.

"Mom and Dad, I want to thank you for everything you've done for me. I'll try very hard every day to make you proud of me in all the endeavors I undertake. Thank you again so much. I could say more, but I think you already know just how I feel."

With that, Christian stood up and walked back through the snow to his family. He took his son and daughter into his arms and asked Ian, Isabelle, and Abigail to lead him to Alexander's grave, which wasn't far away. When they arrived, everyone else stepped back to give Christian a little space. Christian knelt down in the snow, cradling his newborn son and daughter in his arms, and spoke softly so only Alexander and the infants could hear the words.

"Alexander, I want you to meet my son, Alexander Noah, and my daughter, Eilir Elizabeth. I learned that you knew of Abigail's pregnancy before we deployed. You sacrificed everything for me to come home to my family. The only way I can ever repay you is to work at being the best father to my children and the best husband to Abigail I can be. I promise you I will do everything I can so I never let you down."

Christian sobbed on his knees in the snow. Abigail heard him and went to his side. She signaled for her parents to come get the newborns.

"Please wait for us in the car, Mom and Dad," Abigail said.

Ian carried Eilir Elizabeth and Isabelle carried Alexander Noah to the car and buckled them into their infant seats. They slid into their seats and started the car to keep it warm.

Abigail got down on her knees beside Christian and put her arm around him. She kissed him on the cheek and told him she loved him. He dried his eyes and thanked her for her love. "Take your time, Christian. I'll be in the car waiting for you." Abigail stood up and headed for her dad's vehicle.

Christian gathered his thoughts for only a moment, then took a deep breath. "I'm so sorry, Alexander" were the only words he could muster. He bowed his head and closed his eyes.

After a short time, a hand touched Christian on his shoulder and his sadness allayed. He looked up. Above him in the brilliant morning sunlight stood Alexander. If not for Alexander's hand on his shoulder, Christian would have toppled over in the snow from shock.

Before he could ask Alexander any questions, a pulse of energy swept through Christian's body, forcing his eyes to shut. Christian's mind filled with glorious images of heaven, and he heard Alexander's voice saying that everything would be all right. Then Christian knew Alexander was home, safe with the Lord. The energy abated as suddenly as it had come. Christian opened his eyes, but Alexander was gone. Gone, too, were all of Christian's grief and sorrow.

Christian stood up, brushed the snow from his knees, and smiled at Alexander's grave. He turned around, sprinted to the car that had his family inside, and jumped in. Christian smiled to them all as Ian put the car in gear. They all drove off for home, everyone happy, and at peace, save one.

Chapter 26

EPIPHANY

The seconds, bit by bit, ticked by into minutes, and those minutes turned into hours, then days, then weeks. All moved on with their lives, but one soul wasn't entirely at peace. That one was Ian.

Ian's heart had healed and was full of love, but a scar remained where the merciless gash once was. Over the months, he had devoted himself to the Lord and to his family. Still, something nagged at him, the feeling persistent, relentless. Buried deep down in his soul, the thought that his family would never be complete again troubled him. No matter how much he immersed himself in his work and his family, the loss of Alexander was a numbing emptiness that always stayed with him. Ian's feelings, though, were about to change.

On this beautiful August morning, the sky was clear and perfect, the humidity nonexistent. A pleasant breeze circulated the unsullied summer air, and the seventy-five degree temperature promised a quiet, wonderful day. The day was heaven on earth, outside in God's magnificent world.

Ian, however, was oblivious to all of God's glory around him. Instead of enjoying the outdoors on his day off, Ian had hidden himself away inside the safe haven of his church. He sat at his office desk, staring at the date on the calendar. Today would've been the end of Christian and Alexander's one-year tour of duty, the day they would've come home together. Ian closed his eyes, reflecting on the cruelty of it all.

Ian sat all alone, his head hanging low, thinking. He needed quiet time to clear his mind. Today was the day Ian had decided to have the private talk with God he had been putting off since his enlightening encounter with Elizabeth. He had readied himself as best he could. He stood up and slowly made his way to the little chapel in the back of the church.

He shut the chapel doors behind him and locked them. There was no need to turn on the lights. Bright rays of sunlight streamed down through the skylight above, kissing the altar with glorious illumination. The large stained glass window behind the altar painted the chapel in soft shades of blues, reds, yellows, and greens as the sunlight refracted through it. The chapel felt like home to Ian, and he believed he was always safe within its walls. He was ready now, able to face God and question His soul-baffling providence.

Ian walked down the short main aisle and positioned himself between the altar and the stained glass window. He placed his palms on the altar. The Lord's divine light pierced through the skylight, and graced his hands as he steadied himself. Ian looked down for a moment, collecting his thoughts, then looked out to all the empty pews. He smiled as he looked up to the skylight. Then he broke the silence in the room and spoke to God.

"Lord, I've wanted to have this conversation with you for quite some time. But frankly, I still don't know what to say. I've tried so hard to live a good life, a life devoted to serving you. I've tried my hardest to guide people in your love and wisdom. But ever since my encounter with Elizabeth, I have more questions than answers. I feel as if you're trying to send me a deeper message, but I don't understand what it is. Why did any of them have to die, Lord? Why Elizabeth, and Noah, and Alexander? It makes no sense at all to me. I wish you could give me a reason why they had to die."

Ian looked down at the altar for a moment and sifted through his thoughts. Then, with tears building in his eyes, he looked back up to the skylight and avowed, "Lord, I swear to you with my soul, I would do anything to take their places so they could be here experiencing life. All three of them deserve life more than I deserve it." Tears flowed down his cheeks, and he couldn't speak. All the memories of Elizabeth's, Noah's, and Alexander's deaths flooded his mind, heart, and soul. The burden was beyond words.

"Mr. Havily, that's one powerful vow you made to God," a voice spoke from the back of the chapel.

Ian flinched, startled by the unknown voice. Then he saw a man wearing an Army uniform in the shadows.

"Who are you?" Ian squinted through his tears, trying to catch a better look at this man in uniform. "And how did you get in here? I locked the doors!"

The man in uniform didn't answer Ian's question. Instead he said, "Your son knew me as Lieutenant Kabecka, but people know me by many names."

"Please, step into the light so I can see you better."

Lieutenant Kabecka walked up the short aisle and took a seat in the first row of pews.

"My son wrote about you, Lieutenant. He said you were a good man and a good leader."

The Lieutenant smiled. "Your son *is* a good man, Mr. Havily."

"Is? What the hell do you mean by that? My son is dead."

"You *still* don't think that death is final, do you, Ian? I thought Elizabeth's visit would have convinced you otherwise."

Ian took a step forward, confusion sweeping over him, and a hint of anger. "Who the hell are you, Lieutenant? Another angel?"

"I think you know exactly who I am," the Lieutenant said, his voice firm, yet soft and peaceful. "Search your soul and I'm quite sure you will find the answer."

"Are you God?" Ian's hands started to quaver in the presence of this mysterious man.

"Turn around, Ian, and look at the stained glass window." The Lieutenant gestured with a wave of his hand, his silver-gray eyes twinkling like two radiant stars.

Ian spun around and watched the colors of the stained glass window blend together with brilliant illumination. Then a picture emerged, and Ian recognized the ominous setting. Alexander was standing in front of Lieutenant Kabecka, and the Lieutenant had a firm hold on Alexander's arm. The colored image was frozen, like the still frame of a movie.

"What is this, Lieutenant?" Ian didn't turn around; his eyes remained locked on the image of his son.

"This is the moment your son decided to sacrifice his life for Christian's life. You see, this day only Christian was supposed to come home to heaven. Your son convinced me otherwise." Lieutenant Kabecka waved his hand and the movie came alive.

Alexander shouted, "*I'm sorry, sir. I won't obey that order even if you're God himself!*" He clenched his right hand into a fist and punched the Lieutenant square in the nose. The picture froze, then turned back into stained glass. Ian spun around and locked eyes with the Lieutenant's glimmering, silvery-grey eyes.

"That's right, Ian. When Alexander looked into my eyes, he knew I was God. But that didn't matter to your son. He was going out for Christian regardless of my trying to stop him. Your son had made a promise to Abigail that he was going to fulfill. Alexander's love for his family was worth more to him than his own life. For that, I rewarded him with a place in heaven and gave Christian life anew."

"Lord, I know I don't understand your plan sometimes, and I thank you for showing me why my son died. But, I still don't understand why Elizabeth and Noah had to die. And I don't comprehend the message behind the butterfly key. Is it a test or a game?"

The Lieutenant laughed, yet he wasn't mocking Ian. He was trying to comfort him, to calm his fears. "All of life is a test, Ian. All of it."

"Then I want to sacrifice my life to spare my family and Christian's family from their suffering. They deserve life so much more than I ever did. Please, let me be the one to take their place so they can live."

"What makes you think that you are worthy? Need I remind you of your acrimony toward me when your son died? Or how you chose to desecrate your bible by throwing it into the fire?" The Lieutenant stood up and looked into Ian's eyes. "You now have the answers you were searching for, my son. It's time for me to go."

"No!" Ian screamed. He raced down from behind the altar and threw himself at God's feet. "Lord, please! I'll do anything you ask of me. I swear my soul to you. I promise to serve you for the rest of eternity. Please don't leave me like this."

God looked down upon Ian and knew his pain, much like His own Son's pain before his crucifixion. "Stand up, Ian." He put His hands upon the arms of his devoted follower and helped him to his feet. "Very well, my son, your words ring true in your soul. Turn and face the altar."

Ian turned and gazed at the sunlight striking the altar. The room began to shake and the light on the altar burned a bright saffron color. The incandescent light burned hot, and Ian shielded his eyes. Then, the room went silent and still.

Ian looked all around. "What happened?"

"Everything that was, now is not," God replied. "Go to the altar and retrieve your key."

Ian walked to the altar and picked up the butterfly key, the exact key that Elizabeth had given to Christian.

"Now what do I do?"

"Go home and enjoy what will be your final day with your family. You will use the butterfly key today. Once you turn the key, your life on earth will be over. You will receive the sacrifice that you asked for."

Ian cringed a little. "Lord, will my death be painful?"

"If you don't use the key today as I have commanded, you will know the true meaning of hell. Now go home, Ian. Your son and Christian are returning home from war today. Your family is waiting for you."

Ian stood before the Lord, confusion washing over his face.

"Ian, you're wasting your time. Go home before I change my mind."

Ian didn't need to have the Lord tell him again. He slipped the butterfly key into his cassock pocket, rushed out of the church to his car, and drove home. Excitement overcame him as he drove up the driveway and neared the house. Who were the people on his lawn? He came nearer. Could it be? His eyes widened and his jaw dropped in disbelief at the sight before him. Abigail and Isabelle were holding Alexander Noah and Eilir Elizabeth in their arms. Elizabeth and Noah stood next to them. They were alive! Ian parked the car and rushed to put his arms around his dear old friends.

"Are you okay, Ian?" Elizabeth asked.

"I'm fine. You and Noah look terrific to me."

The reunion was a joyous, amazing experience for Ian's battered soul. He was so thankful God had given his old friends life, and given him the opportunity to see the miracle.

Abigail pointed toward the driveway. "Here they come!"

Ian turned to see Christian's truck coming up the gravel driveway. His stomach churned as he watched the truck come to a halt. Both doors swung open, and Christian and Alexander stepped out. Ian rushed over and hugged his son for a long while, holding him as tight as he could.

"I'm home, Dad." Alexander patted his father on the back, then went over and hugged his mom.

Ian looked up to heaven and smiled. "Thank you, Lord." He turned and watched Christian and Alexander hug the rest of the family, and the sight warmed his soul. Ian walked over to his wife and Abigail and hugged them and his grandchildren.

"Are you all right, Dad?" Abigail asked.

Ian smiled. "I'm fine, Abigail, just fine."

"Oh, Dad, before I forget, a package was dropped off for you. I put it on your desk."

Ian didn't say a word. He knew it was time to fulfill his promise to God. Knowing what now must be done, he flashed his daughter a faint smile and walked into the house.

Ian went into his office and shut the door behind him. He sat down at his desk and stared at the package before him. He opened it and pulled out the butterfly chest. Ian took the butterfly key from his cassock pocket, moved the gold flap, and slid the butterfly key into the lock. He looked to the ceiling and prayed for God to grant him the strength to turn the butterfly key. "A promise is a promise," he muttered aloud. Ian closed his eyes and turned the key counterclockwise until it clicked. He opened his right eye first, then his left. Nothing had happened. He took a deep breath and opened the chest.

The moment he lifted the lid, a blinding, burning white light escaped from the chest and encompassed Ian's body. He shook violently, but for only a moment. When the light abated, Ian's glassy eyes rolled back in his head. He slumped over in his chair and didn't move again. With his promise to God fulfilled, the butterfly key and the butterfly chest evanesced from this world, and Ian's soul departed as well.

Epilogue

As I finished the allegory of the Havily and Bryson families, I looked at my wife and three daughters. I had to smile at my littlest one, Chloe, fast asleep on her mother's lap. My smile was quick to wash out, however, when I heard the complaints of my wife and other two daughters. They were none too happy with me for the story's ending.

"Dad, how come Ian had to die?" Ashley and Emma asked in unison.

"Yeah, why did Ian have to die? That's way too heartbreaking," my wife said, frowning.

"I'm sorry, but Ian sacrificed his life for the lives of three people he loved with all of his heart. I think that's a fair trade," I said, glancing at the large clock on the wall.

It was late, time for my brood to head off to bed. I picked up Chloe and carried her to her bed and tucked her in. After giving her a kiss goodnight, I did the same with the two older girls. "Sweet dreams, Ashley. Sweet dreams, Emma," I said, turning off their bedroom light.

My wife had already made her way to bed, so I changed into my flannel pajamas, crawled in beside her, and gave her a goodnight kiss. She rolled over on her side and I nestled up behind her.

"That was a beautiful story you told us tonight, my love. But I wish you'd reconsider the ending. I think it's too tragic, and I don't think God would have let it end that way."

"I'll think about it," I replied softly. I then started to rub my wife's tummy in small, gentle circles. This seemed to help her fall asleep much easier, ever since the miscarriage of our baby. "Now get some sleep, my love. I'm pretty sure the kids will be up early in the morning wanting to open Christmas presents." Before long, we were both fast asleep.

At two in the morning, I abruptly woke from my deep slumber. My pajamas were soaked with sweat, and I vividly recalled the heartrending dream I had just envisioned. My heart ached, and my soul was crushed as I sat up. With cat-like stealth I moved out of bed and went into my walk-in closet, located a pair of dry pajamas in the dark, then tiptoed through the bedroom and into the bathroom to not disturb my sleeping wife.

The shower felt invigorating. Still, my mind raced like a hamster on a wheel. I toweled off with haste, put on my dry pajamas, and crawled back into bed with my wife.

"Is everything okay?" she asked.

"It will be in the morning, my love," I whispered. "Go back to sleep."

I held my wife in my arms and we both slept until eight. We awoke to the sound of our three daughters knocking on our bedroom door.

"They're late this morning," I said to my wife. We sat up and smiled at one another.

"Come in," my wife called to them.

Our daughters flew through the doorway, climbed into our king-sized bed, and snuggled up to us. "Merry Christmas," they giggled, squeezing us tight.

"Merry Christmas," my wife and I replied.

I kissed and hugged each one of my beautiful daughters and then gazed at my stunning wife, my eyes twinkling.

"What is it?" my wife asked. She always knew when I had something on my mind.

I cleared my throat and smiled. "God stood, magnificent yet indiscernible, before Ian's lifeless body slumped in his office chair. He looked down on Ian with immense compassion and forgiveness in his almighty eyes. God placed his ethereal hands on Ian's head, gracing him with love. Ian's body violently jolted back to life, and he gasped for air. All of the memories Ian had experienced over his lifetime were now gone, erased by God. The recollections that once flooded Ian's mind, both good and bad, emptied away, like the last grains of sand in an hourglass. But God always has a plan. For Ian, God turned over the hourglass and filled his mind with all the memories that this new life held. Ian stood up and looked around the room. He experienced something wonderful deep within his mind and soul: peace. His life was now full of purpose, his path made clear by God. Ian left the office and joined his family outside. The Havilys and the Brysons would live the happy lives of those who are truly blessed."

My children squealed in delight, and my wife hugged and kissed me. Everyone was jubilant! Ian was now alive!

"Thank you," my wife said.

"Thank you for what?" I asked.

"For helping me find my faith in God again."

I smiled at all my beautiful girls, then spoke the magic words: "Let's go open the Christmas presents." My daughters gave a happy yelp and ran out of our bedroom and into the living room. Laughing at their uncontainable excitement, my wife and I were quick to join them.

We sat on the couch as our daughters passed out the gifts, and I watched, thankful for the presents my wife and kids would open.

Now, when it comes to gifts, I'm adamant: I need nothing, preferring to have any money spent on my wife and kids or to purchase a gift for the whole family. This year, however, someone decided to risk all, tempting their fate and luck by giving me a present.

I looked at the box wrapped in ruby-red paper and gold ribbon, with a thick white envelope on top. "Okay, who broke the rules and bought me a gift?" I demanded to know.

Denials all around.

Frowning, I pulled the envelope off the box. It was addressed to me, all right, but I didn't recognize the handwriting. With everyone watching, I opened the envelope. My stomach dropped as I opened the letter and found a beautiful, ornate orange and black butterfly key inside. I looked at each member of my family, but it quickly became apparent that none of them had anything to do with this gift.

"What does the letter say?" my wife asked.

My hands trembled as I read the words aloud...

I loved your story, and I am pleased with the way you decided to end it this morning. Please use this butterfly key to find the gifts from me to your family. May your hearts never stop believing in your faith.

Sincerely,
Lieutenant Kabecka

I looked over to my wife, who was in just as much shock as I was. The kids urged me to open the box, so I slowly peeled away the wrapping paper. Underneath, I discovered a butterfly chest. My hands were shaking hard so my wife had to use the butterfly key to open the chest for me. Inside was a leather journal, a Monarch butterfly embroidered on the cover. Within, all the pages were blank, but I now knew my purpose. It was to write the improbable story I just narrated to my wife and kids and share it with others.

Also inside the butterfly chest were several beautiful, colorful, crystal Monarch butterfly barrettes, one for each one of my girls.

"There are five of them," my wife said.

I furrowed my brow while I thought. I had a wife and three daughters. Who was the fifth butterfly barrette for? Then it struck me. I looked to my wife and struggled to speak. My mouth was all cottony inside.

"What is it?" she asked.

"Do you have any pregnancy tests left?"

"Yes, but why?"

"I think you'd better go take it. I believe the fifth butterfly barrette is intended for another child."

My wife raced to the bathroom and locked the door. I waited and waited, pacing the floor at a feverish clip. Finally, after several long, excruciating minutes, she emerged from the bathroom, trembling, with tears in her beautiful blue eyes, and whispered only a couple wonderful words: "I'm pregnant."

I held my crying wife tight, secure in my arms. Humbled by her words, I looked up to heaven and whispered, "Thank you, Lord," for I had received the best Christmas gift anyone could ever hope for.

Postscript

I'm sure there are people in this world who will call this story spectacularly unbelievable, and to be honest, I couldn't blame them. But those people who possess the unique gift of listening with their hearts just might find it a wonderful miracle. All I have to do is look into my wife's beautiful eyes and I know that what other people think really doesn't matter. Her faith in God is no longer in question, and to me, that is the best miracle of all.

Breinigsville, PA USA
30 August 2010
244523BV00001B/2/P